Coming Home for Us

The Wilder Brothers
Book 4

Carrie Ann Ryan

COMING HOME FOR US

A WILDER BROTHERS NOVEL

By

Carrie Ann Ryan

COMING HOME FOR US
A Wilder Brothers Novel
By: Carrie Ann Ryan
© 2022 Carrie Ann Ryan
eBook ISBN 978-1-63695-183-6
Paperback ISBN 978-1-63695-184-3
Cover Art by Sweet N Spicy Designs
Photo by Wander Aguiar Photography

Praise for Carrie Ann Ryan

"Count on Carrie Ann Ryan for emotional, sexy, character driven stories that capture your heart!" – Carly Phillips, NY Times bestselling author

"Carrie Ann Ryan's romances are my newest addiction! The emotion in her books captures me from the very beginning. The hope and healing hold me close until the end. These love stories will simply sweep you away." ~ NYT Bestselling Author Deveny Perry

"Carrie Ann Ryan writes the perfect balance of sweet and heat ensuring every story feeds the soul." - Audrey Carlan, #1 New York Times Bestselling Author

"Carrie Ann Ryan never fails to draw readers in with passion, raw sensuality, and characters that pop off the page. Any book by Carrie Ann is an absolute treat." – New York Times Bestselling Author J. Kenner

"Carrie Ann Ryan knows how to pull your heartstrings and make your pulse pound! Her wonderful Redwood Pack series will draw you in and keep you reading long into the night. I can't wait to see what comes next with the new generation, the Talons. Keep them coming, Carrie Ann!" –Lara Adrian, New York Times bestselling author of CRAVE THE NIGHT

"With snarky humor, sizzling love scenes, and brilliant, imaginative worldbuilding, The Dante's Circle series reads as if Carrie Ann Ryan peeked at my personal wish list!" – NYT Bestselling Author, Larissa Ione

"Carrie Ann Ryan writes sexy shifters in a world full of passionate happily-ever-afters." – *New York Times* Bestselling Author Vivian Arend

"Carrie Ann's books are sexy with characters you can't help but love from page one. They are heat and heart blended to perfection." *New York Times* Bestselling Author Jayne Rylon

Carrie Ann Ryan's books are wickedly funny and deliciously hot, with plenty of twists to keep you guessing. They'll keep you up all night!" USA Today Bestselling Author Cari Quinn

"Once again, Carrie Ann Ryan knocks the Dante's Circle series out of the park. The queen of hot, sexy, enthralling paranormal romance, Carrie Ann is an author not to miss!" *New York Times* bestselling Author Marie Harte

COMING HOME FOR US

The Wilder Brothers from NYT Bestselling Author Carrie Ann Ryan continue with Elijah's last chance at redemption and love.

I made plans. I followed the path. I fell in love.

Then the world took her away from me.

I swore to never love again, and I've done all I could to keep that vow.

But life finds a way and I can't stop this burning attraction with my best friend.

Maddie stood by me when my world shattered.

She deserves more than a broken man who promised to never love again.

Only I swear she feels the same way about me. And I have no idea what to do about it.

Now she might leave the Wilders and I can't tell her to

stay—even if it means shattering the one piece of me I have left.

To Dan.
I miss you.

Chapter One

Maddie

When my phone began to chirp with notifications in rapid, staccato bursts, I knew my morning would end in shambles. I paused my yoga program on my laptop, slid out of downward dog awkwardly, and then picked up my phone. It continued to buzz, one right after another, and I cursed myself for setting my notifications to alerts, sound, vibrations, and flash. Before this job with the Wilders, I had been able to hide from all social media and email notifications. I had been able to decide whether I wanted to check those little red boxes on my phone or not. Now, though, I needed to know immediately what was going on. I was the wine club and tasting manager of Wilder Wines. Meaning people needed to know where I was, and I needed to be on top of things. Only as my phone did its own little break dance across my hardwood floors I winced.

No, today was not going to be a good day.

I sat down cross-legged on the floor, rolled my shoulders back, and figured that half of a workout was at least decent.

I looked at the screen, and my eyes closed.

Seventy-four new messages.

I had just checked my email earlier and everything had been labeled and set in the correct folders for priority, while eating quick overnight oats with my coffee before I worked out. I wasn't one of those people that could just wake up and do things without food in my stomach. No, even half-blurry, one-eye open, still crust in that eye, I needed food in my stomach.

I was the exact opposite of all of my friends, but it didn't matter. I knew my routine, so I checked my email while doing that, and now I was supposed to be enjoying a nice relaxing workout, only it didn't seem to be that way.

I opened up the first email and cursed.

"Are you kidding me? Seriously? No. Someone couldn't be that stupid."

But they were.

A local business had cc'd instead of bcc'd three hundred or so people a confidential email. One that had to do with a wine club festival we were trying to be invited to.

Oh, dear God.

And it wasn't just that he had cc'd instead of blind copied. Now we could all see each other's emails, could see who was on this list, who wasn't, and who was important enough to be considered.

The next email, of course, was an apology, this time a blind copy which didn't negate the fact that he had already ruined the day for so many of us—including himself.

Because now the worst was happening.

Not just the confidential email with contract language and introductions. All of those things needed to be personalized and hidden.

No, it wasn't that. It wasn't even the fact that now all other businesses that might not understand consent were going to have our email addresses and there was going to be no getting out of that.

No, it was even far worse.

The first email was the dreaded *reply all*.

Not just to reply to him to let him know that he had sent the wrong email to everybody. Or that it was, *yes, I got it,* or an acknowledgment. Professional or laid back, it didn't matter.

Oh, all of those were in there.

And they were *reply all*.

I groaned as my phone continued to vibrate. One message after another.

Thank you. Got it!

Awesome. See you soon.

Oh wow, I didn't realize it was that date.

Did you send the right attachment? Thank you!

On it.

Acknowledged.

K.

Hey, stop using reply all everybody. Reply all means we all get it.

The irony that that person replied all to that did not escape my notice. Nor the notice of the fifteen replies that reply all-ed to that man to explain it.

It was going to be a long day. Because as each person emailed back a reply all, other people took it on themselves to reply all to that reply all.

I was going to need a drink before this day was over. Luckily, I worked at a winery. However, it didn't seem like there was going to be enough wine on the planet for this.

I stood up and stretched my back. I knew that no amount of yoga was going to fix this.

Instead, I took my vibrating phone to the restroom with me and quickly showered. It continued to buzz as it sat on the ledge in my shower, and I glanced through soapy eyes to see if it was anything important. It would take a lot of effort to weed through my emails to find legitimate ones because people were idiots and hadn't kept the subject line the same. So instead of all of the emails being embedded on one line, they took up and ever expanding amount of space.

And it just kept going. It was never going to end.

I finished showering, wrapped my hair in a towel, and proceeded to lotion, pluck, and get ready for my day. I wish I could be one of those people that just wore jeans and a T-shirt at work. A lot of my friends who worked on the vines and within the company were able to do that. One of my best friends, Kendall, could just wrap a chef's coat around whatever she wore and be fine.

But I was one of the faces of the Wilder Retreat. Which, considering I was one of the few of my friends not married into the Wilders, made it a little odd.

When the Wilders retired from the military, each for various reasons that I still didn't know and it wasn't my business, they bought the Retreat and Winery.

From the outside, it seemed as if they had lost their damn minds. None of them knew anything about wedding venues, owning a company like this, and they sure as hell didn't know anything about wine. It turned out that Elijah and Evan both knew a little bit about wine because of their family connections, but when I first met them I was really afraid I was about to lose my job and end up penniless, or spend all of my time being mansplained to while having to teach them.

Thankfully, it had been nothing like that, and in the years we had worked together, we'd become a family, a powerhouse on the wedding and winery circuit outside San Antonio, Texas.

I knew that they could have done anything and succeeded. Whatever the Wilders wanted, they got, because they worked their asses off for it.

Well, at least most things they got, but I didn't want to think about that familiar pain.

It had been two years since the Wilders had lost one of their own. Since I had lost one of my good friends. A woman I didn't think I was going to like at first because of who she loved. And who loved her. But Joy had been my friend, and it still hurt to think about her, because one of my best friends was dead. Gone. And the man she had loved was still sort of my boss.

And that was all he was. At least anymore.

I shook my head at those morose thoughts, and quickly dried my hair, grateful for my new blow dryer that did it in a quarter of the time now, so I didn't have to wake up before the sun rose to get it done.

My hair used to stop right above my butt, with slight waves and caramel highlights, but I recently chopped it to just above my shoulders, and I liked the look. It was different, but it worked for me. At least, I hoped it did. My boyfriend thought it did, so I counted that as a win. Not that I'd seen my boyfriend often in the past few weeks. Time and messy schedules meant we were two ships passing in the night, not actually seeing each other, but maybe that would change soon.

I finished my makeup and went through my notes for the day, making sure that I was ready for what was coming up. I had two wine tours and a club meeting.

Wine clubs bought our wine and helped us sell it. Between that, and hopefully this upcoming festival, despite how these emails started out, we were putting Wilders on the map. Wilder Wines was a thing now, and not just a hobby for six brothers.

I was damn good at my job, at meeting people, at making sure that they were having the best time. And I sold wine like nobody's business. Elijah and Evan could make it, along with their winemakers, but I sold it.

My phone buzzed again and I groaned, but did that little heart skip when I realized it was Elijah's name on the email. I cursed that little blip because damn it, it shouldn't be doing that anymore.

I didn't love him anymore. Not that I had *really* loved him. But I'd had that heart crush, where you knew that that person could be the one for you. Where every connection and every breath just made sense. But he never saw me that way. And I knew for a fact he never realized that I wanted him as anything other than his friend and coworker.

It had taken realizing that he was in love with another woman, and we were better off as friends, for me to finally just move on. I didn't love him that way, and while he was attractive as hell, I didn't have that pull anymore. No more spark.

7

I even had two failed relationships in the past two years. While Elijah had been in mourning, grief overriding everything he did, I had tried my best to find love. Hadn't really figured it out yet, but Nathaniel, my boyfriend, gave me some spark. We were comfortable, and I was happy.

I might be a little restless, but it had nothing to do with the Wilders, nothing to do with Nathaniel and love, and everything to do with me.

I had been working with the Wilders since they opened the resort over four years ago, and I didn't know if this was my last stop or just a stepping stone. That was something I was going to have to figure out on my own, though.

But thankfully, I knew it had nothing to do with Elijah. Although, every once in a while, when I wasn't expecting it, seeing his name on an email or even in a text did something to me. But it was out of habit, a ghost reflex, nothing more.

From: Elijah
To: Maddie
Subject: RE: are they serious?
I snorted. Apparently, he was one of the ones who changed the subject lines.
Are they serious right now with all these emails? Did none of them go to business school? No, did any of them learn how to use email at any point in their

life. Don't they know that there are memes about
reply all at this point? Who the hell uses reply all?

I laughed and picked up my phone to reply back.

From: Maddie
To: Elijah
Subject: RE:RE: are they serious?
Oh, they are serious. Because they need to make
sure everybody else knows that they know that reply
alls are wrong. Or they're just stupid. None of them
have actually said anything important. And I haven't
had time to go over the original email. But I'm interested to see whatever this festival brings us. If we
even get invited. For all I know, he just sent out a
mass email saying you all suck we're not doing the
festival, and we're going to move on to French wines,
not local ones.

I'll be in soon. And we can talk about it then.
But I do have a question though—did you feel like
replying all? Or just to me?

I frowned and erased that last line. There was no reason for that. It was a little too personal. We were friends, and he had no problem talking to me about most things. But I knew if I wanted to remain sane, I needed to keep some boundaries. Even if it felt a little weird.

I grabbed my bag and got into my car so I could head to the Wilder property—my home away from home.

When the Wilders first opened their business, many of them lived on site. Not everybody did anymore. When Eli and Alexis got married and subsequently had their daughter Kylie, they moved into a house they had built. Evan and Kendall and their twins Reese and Cassie all lived offsite as well. Everett and his girlfriend, one of my favorite superstars ever, Bethany Cole, lived offsite when they were in the area, and split their time between here and LA. In the two years since they had finally gotten together, they had found this weird balance where it felt like Everett was always here because he was constantly on emails and video chats with us, even while they were in LA for her work. I didn't know how the brothers felt about that, considering the whole point of owning this business was for them to get to know each other and come together, but I liked the fact that Everett was happy. He deserved it. All of the Wilder brothers did.

And I deserved it too, though I wasn't sure why I had that weird thought.

I lived offsite as well, but I always had. I had a small house about twenty minutes from the Wilder Retreat and

Winery, which in Texas was only just down the road. Everything was big in Texas, therefore getting anywhere took all damn day.

I pulled in past the new security gates and nodded at the staffer. He nodded back and checked my license plate. I kept moving because I worked there and they knew me well enough I didn't have to sign in. But guests did, and while I knew that some winery guests and residents might not enjoy it, they got used to it. Many companies and businesses did that these days, because it kept people safer, and I for one was happy for that. With everything that had happened to my friends over the past few years, we needed that safety net.

And Trace, Bethany's bodyguard, had helped set up everything for us.

I waved at the car going the opposite way and grinned, thinking about how things had changed.

Trace had come to us thanks to Bethany, and the person driving away, LJ, was now our contract lawyer. He had his own business, and had once worked for our rival company, but through a series of events that still made my heart hurt, LJ was now family, in the same way that I was family.

I pulled into my spot, waved at a few people as I got out of the car, but kept walking.

"Maddie," a voice called out.

I turned to see Jay, our vintner and winemaker. He was broad-shouldered like the Wilders, but a little shorter, not as muscular. He worked hard, was a brilliant wine-maker, and had been my friend longer than the Wilders had.

"Hey there."

"I saw you in the email. Not all the Wilders got it, but you, me, and Elijah. We're the great ones."

I rolled my eyes. "Great. So happy we can wallow in our pain together."

"Amos wasn't on it, though. Which was surprising."

Amos was our vineyard manager and was surly, growly, and I wasn't surprised he wasn't on the email. He got things done, but on his own terms. However, that was fine with me. As long as the other people didn't have to deal with his growliness, that meant I could get more work done.

"Hopefully, the emails stop soon."

"That's always the goal. You have a first tasting up this morning, 10:00 a.m., wine. That makes me happy."

I grinned. "After all those emails, I'll probably do the tasting with them."

"Do strong pours. It's what we like." He winked, handed off a stack of notes for me, and I thanked him before heading back to my office.

I looked up at another call of my name and smiled.

My heart didn't do that little twisting pitter-pat thing. But it did warm. Because I knew this man. And I wanted to love him.

My boyfriend Nathaniel jogged up to me, cupped my face, and kissed me softly.

"Hey there."

I smiled back. "Hi. I didn't know you were going to be here today."

"I'm meeting Eli and Alexis later to go over something for the setlist."

Nathaniel was in a band, though that wasn't his day job. His main job was working numbers for a local business, but he moonlighted in a band that did gigs for the Wilders. It was how we had met. He had played a song and sung just to me, and I had laughed and then danced with him when the DJ went on for a bit.

Alexis and Kendall had pushed me towards saying yes to a date and, knowing that I needed to move on from yet another failed relationship, I did.

Nathaniel could be a rock star, he was growly, and suave, and it was enough.

"I'm glad that you're here."

"I'm glad that I'm here too. What do you say to dinner tonight?" he asked, his voice low. He wiggled his brows and I laughed.

"Is that your line?"

"Hey, we both work at least two jobs. Sometimes my line has to be a wiggle of my brows."

"You know what, you're right. We're not kids anymore. As long as you don't ask me if I fell from heaven or whatever that line is, I'm fine."

"I've got you, babe." He kissed me hard, and I pushed at him.

"I'm working, Nathaniel."

"True true."

He looked over my shoulder and grinned. "Hey, there's your boss."

I turned because the hairs on the back of my neck had already stood on end. I had known Elijah was there.

I always did.

That was the damn problem.

"Hello, you two. I see you're manhandling my wine club manager."

"Only in the best ways," Nathaniel said as he hugged me to his side.

I rolled my eyes and pushed at him. "Okay. I do actually have to get to work."

"I figured, with all the emails," Elijah said with a roll of his eyes.

The fact that he looked happy and was laughing a bit meant everything to me. Because in the past two years, he hadn't. Before losing Joy, he had always had a little spark in his eyes, a little grin. He'd been suave and jovial, and a little growly when he needed to be, but he always smiled. He'd always made anyone feel like they were the center of the universe, even for that one conversation.

Then he lost the love of his life, and had grown dark, cold. Now it looked as if he might be clawing back out of that abyss, and that meant everything to me, because I wanted him to have the best.

He needed it.

"Email thing?" Nathaniel asked, with a frown on his face.

"Don't worry. It's just a work thing. I'll see you later tonight, though. Yes, to dinner."

"Sounds good, babe." He kissed me on the forehead and then held out his fist to Elijah. "Did you see the Stars?"

I frowned. "The stars? Like up there?" I asked him and pointed at the sky.

The guys looked at each other and then sighed.

"Hockey," they said at the same time.

I threw my free hand up in the air. "I like sports. I just don't understand the idea of hockey in Texas."

"It's an indoor rink," Elijah explained. "They keep it chilled inside. They aren't playing on ice in the heat."

"And after a hot day, playing inside where it's cold is fun," Nathaniel added.

I shook my head, wondering why it felt so weird that these two seemed to be friends, or at least friendly. It shouldn't matter.

"Okay, you guys, I'm going to work. You guys talk about your sportsball."

"You say that as if you're not a hardcore New Orleans Saints fan," Elijah teased.

Nathaniel sighed. "I still can't believe it."

"Who dat?" I laughed and left them alone, shaking my head as I looked at my email again.

They continued to talk about sports and I just ignored them, knowing that I needed to focus on my day and not the countless emails that kept popping into my inbox.

But one email was there.

One email I wasn't ready to think about.

I knew what it was.

I wasn't a Wilder. I wasn't tied to this place irrevocably. And I needed something. Something more. I was damn good at my job. I thrived at this.

Only I hadn't changed what I was doing in the past three years. And I didn't know what I was supposed to do. I ignored the email in my inbox, though I would have to deal with it soon.

I wasn't a Wilder. I wasn't wild.

But maybe, just maybe, it was time to move on.

Chapter Two

Elijah

Soft hands slid down my chest, over the cotton of my shirt, before thin fingers wrapped around my belt loops and pulled me close. I laughed, not hearing exactly what she was saying but knowing it was to the heart. And when she pressed her lips to mine, I sank into them, warmth and heat and pressure. Gentle. Not too much, Not too little.

I opened my eyes and looked down into her bright ones, but I couldn't remember the exact color of her eyes. Or the shade of her hair. But I knew that kind smile because she radiated her name.

Joy.

"You've been gone two years now. I don't know why I keep dreaming like this. It's probably not good for me."

She shook her head and pulled me closer. We were pressed body to body, front to front, but I couldn't feel her. I knew once again this was a dream.

"I always hated my name. I think I told you that."

She had—multiple times. But she always laughed it off and made a pun. Just like we joked about the fact that I shared the same letter of my first name with all six of my siblings. My family had never been able to get our names right, and Joy had been a joy. Until the world took that from me. Or perhaps that was a selfish way to think about it. Because she was taken from the world, not just me. But in this moment I just wanted to be selfish, for a bare instant, I would tell myself that she was taken from me alone. And that was why this pain ebbed but never went away.

She was gone.

I didn't know how to bring her back.

I knew that was never going to happen anyway.

But we had these dreams.

"You need to wake up. You have a long day. And thinking of me isn't going to help."

"True. But I like thinking of you."

She smiled, her eyes going gray, hazy. "You loved me. You were in love with me. Are you still?"

I didn't want to answer that, so I wouldn't. It didn't seem fair. My subconscious was being a real bitch today.

Usually, these dreams were a little too real, and I didn't know that I was dreaming until I woke up, my body sweat-slick, tears streaming down my face, and Joy not lying next to me.

This time it felt like an out-of-body experience, and I didn't know what she wanted from me.

"Wake up now. And think about that. I don't want you to hate your future. Not because of me."

I let out a hollow laugh, aware that my waking would break me out of this any moment. "I made that vow. I had you. Even for a minute. Though you never wore my ring."

"Only a few moments too late. I would have said yes, you know."

Joy died walking across the street while I waited for her. I had sat in the restaurant for over an hour, panicked, hoping she was just running late, but she hadn't answered her phone. Her parents had been her emergency contact in her phone, and they called me. I had heard the sirens, the ambulance. But I hadn't even thought it could be her. That only two blocks away—because she hadn't been able to find a place to park on the street—the woman that I loved more than life had died.

The authorities hadn't told Joy's parents or me if she had died instantly or if she had tried to call for help. All I knew was that the car had been speeding in the rain, had slid and hydroplaned, slamming right into her.

I didn't know about her last moments, although I had dreams about all the possibilities.

Dreams that never went away.

"Am I just telling myself you would have said yes? Because you're not you, Joy. You're just the memory of the woman I love."

"Present tense? Still?"

"Should I quote my favorite semi-villain and say always?" I asked softly.

"I think you need to think a little harder. But wake up. It's time to wake up."

My eyes opened, and once again, Joy wasn't next to me.

The ring box that I had held that night, waiting for her to arrive so I could propose like she had always wanted, sat in my nightstand drawer.

It was buried under a few things now, because I didn't pull it out to look at every night like I had before. I used to sit on the side of the bed, my head hanging, looking down at the ring that Joy had never seen. That she had never worn.

My dreams told me that she would have said yes, and I had hoped she would, but I would never know because I hadn't had the chance to ask.

Joy was gone. Dead. What was I supposed to do with that?

Perhaps nothing. Perhaps everything.

My hands itched to reach for my nightstand drawer to look at the ring again, but it wouldn't help.

I was never going to ask her to marry me. And in the

two years that I had through those stages of grief, I had come to terms with that.

Joy had been the best moments of my life, and now she was gone. But I still had work to do. A family to take care of. A business to run. And a life to lead.

Though Joy wouldn't be at my side for all of that, I could still survive. I might not ever find that happiness again, but I was okay with who I was. It had taken me these years to figure that out. I enjoyed being Uncle Elijah, a brother to my family, a brother-in-law to the women and man who had joined us. That was all I needed.

I stretched, rubbed the back of my neck, and wished that I could have a little more sleep, but that wasn't going to happen.

Instead, I walked towards the bathroom and jumped into the shower, letting the scalding hot water beat into my skin, reminding me that I was still here. I had only imagined feeling Joy in those dreams. As she hadn't been there. But this I could feel. This I could breathe through.

This was why I was here.

I got ready for work quickly and looked down at my phone, my emails still a little staggering. Thankfully the reply alls of yesterday's disaster was trickling away.

My lips still twitched, thinking about my emails with Maddie. We had continued emailing throughout the day, complaining about the others, though we did talk about work. We worked well together. I wouldn't be able to do what I did without her.

I was the operations director for Wilder Wines. I set the strategy for the winery and made sure that we were looking toward the future. My brother Evan was the wine-making director. He was in charge of the people who made our wines, along with our vintner and other directors. They produced the product that I helped sell with Maddie.

We were a team.

I slid into my suit, feeling far more comfortable than I had a right to be. I didn't always wear a suit for work, but I liked to. I liked the feel of the fabric against my skin and the way it made me look. I liked that it had nothing to do with my previous life.

Out of all of my siblings, I had always felt I was the least suited to military life. I joined because I hadn't known what else to do. I had been enlisted, without a college degree, later using the GI Bill for a business degree. I had been a meteorologist for the Air Force, so I didn't even have the same experiences that my brothers had. I worked hard, long hours, and without me, bases were in danger. It wasn't just the threat of the enemy, but the world that wanted to fight back after we tried to destroy it.

My job was important, a small but vital cog in the machine. I didn't even have a meteorology degree. That's not how things worked in the Air Force. Then, when I got out, I hadn't wanted to be a meteorologist. I had been set on that path by others, and it didn't suit me. When Eli had come to me with an idea, I'd clung to it because I'd had nothing else, and I'd missed my family.

Once I put on the suit, I wasn't Staff Sergeant Wilder anymore. I was Elijah Wilder, kick-ass-boss, according to Maddie and my sisters-in-law. I chuckled, the action a little rusty. I wasn't good at remembering how to laugh, but the girls were making sure that I didn't forget. I pulled out my phone, thought about shooting a quick email to Maddie, and frowned. I didn't have anything to say to her about work yet. I didn't know how today was going to go. And yet the first thing I had thought of was emailing her. Weird. It must have just been the odd day off yesterday. I had liked that email chain, because it was different than the monotony of life. Or perhaps I just needed coffee. And because I was thinking about it, I quickly poured myself a cup from my automated machine and headed to my golf cart. I lived on the property, though some of my brothers didn't. Thanks to the luck of the draw, actual straws being drawn, I had the largest house on the property. I liked it and didn't have any plans to move. At one point, I thought Joy might move in with me, but that hadn't been fate's plan, and I was finally getting the idea through my head.

I could have walked, but I went for a run last night until my legs had practically fallen off, and I was still a little sore. I would run myself to sleep again tonight, but for now I took the golf cart, and smiled at any of our staff or guests that happened to be on the property.

The Wilder Retreat was just that. A place for people to come and enjoy a nice evening with five-star cuisine, fresh sheets, and the little delicacies that came with being cared for. Our time in the service had brought us a great appreciation for those creature comforts that we might not otherwise have indulged.

Alexis was our wedding planner, and we had brought her in after we had gone through a couple of wedding planners of our own, and not only had she married my brother and taken our name, but had put Wilder Weddings on the map.

Now we had a waiting list for people to get onto our property, not just for weddings, but for retirements and special events. Alexis handled the weddings personally, while my youngest brother Elliot handled all the other events. I wasn't sure exactly how he dealt with that on a daily basis, but they were both kicking ass, and I was proud of them.

Eli and Everett handled everything else on that end, while Everett also made sure that we didn't go bankrupt.

Evan and I handled the winery, while East handled everything else. He was our handyman and resident builder. Elliot had wanted East to have another title, something a little fancier than a handyman, but East had punched him playfully, growled, and stomped away.

So East was our handyman, and we made sure we

made a lot of "what went into his hands" jokes all the time. We were brothers, after all.

I pulled into the winery, nodding at Amos, who was talking with Jay. The two would come to me if they needed me, but they mostly worked with Evan, while I worked with Maddie.

I went through my phone as I headed to my office, but I nearly tripped over my feet.

I opened the email and grinned.

"Heck yeah!" I said, punching the air.

Maddie came forward, clipboard in hand, and raised a brow.

"Everything okay?"

I looked at her then and frowned. "Did you cut your hair?"

She blinked at me and rolled her eyes. "Last week. But thank you for noticing."

"It's down now. You usually have it up. You could have cut it last year for all I remember."

"I do get haircuts often if that helps. But yes, I cut my hair." She shrugged and ran her hand through it. "What do you think?"

I wasn't quite sure what I was supposed to say. She wasn't technically my employee because she worked under Evan and not me. Which was good because we tended to growl at each other. We worked better when we were butting heads, but that meant that Evan was her boss and not me.

However, even mentioning her hair was probably weird.

"You look like you."

That sounded fine. Right?

She just stared at me, then shrugged. "Sure. That works. Anyway, good email?"

I wanted to tell her—she had a right to know—but first, I had to tell my brothers because there were plans involved that they needed to be aware of. So I just smiled. "Yes. I've got to get back to Evan. You okay for the day?"

She gave me a look. "Yes. Will you let me know if you need me?" She paused. "For work."

"Of course I will." I nearly frowned as she looked at me, wondering what I'd said wrong.

I didn't know why she was so awkward with me right then. She didn't used to be. But then again, we had a couple of weird years. I relied on Maddie, so did Evan. But sometimes, I felt as if she were far too big for this company. That was why the meeting that I had with my brothers was so important.

Usually, we met over at the inn in our business center, but another company was having a retreat at the inn, so they had the business center reserved. We were meeting in the employee wine-tasting room, though it was far too early in the morning to do a tasting, but I knew Kendall had promised us pastries. And that was all that mattered.

My brothers were there, as were Alexis and Kendall. All of us were partners in our business. Although Alexis and Kendall hadn't been originally, they bought their way in, and not just because they were now Wilders. They wanted to be part of the company, and over the past two years, we restructured to make that happen.

And with my email's possible good news, that meant the next phase could happen soon. If she said yes after all. But why wouldn't she?

East glanced up at me from his place near the food and grunted.

"Late night?"

He raised a brow and stuffed a mini quiche in his mouth.

"Okay then. You don't have to answer."

"Plumbing issue at cabin four," Elliot said with a shrug as he slid between us and popped a quiche in his mouth.

"Are you guys planning on chewing those?" Kendall asked as she rearranged her work.

I leaned forward and kissed my sister-in-law on her cheek, and she batted her eyelashes at me.

"Good morning, handsome."

"Hands off my wife," Evan called out.

"Never." I hugged Kendall close to me, and I didn't miss the look passing between my brothers.

Yes, I knew I had been a grouchy asshole recently, much like East was most of the time, but I was trying to be better. I didn't need to be the sad boyfriend anymore. Joy was gone, she wasn't coming back, but I didn't need to be pitied.

So I was going to try to be better.

"Well then. I'll have what you're having," Kendall said with a laugh, and I wiggled my brows again before Evan stole her away.

"We are here for a business meeting, Elijah. Act your age."

"I am acting my age. Thank you very much."

"Plumbing problem fixed?" Eli asked East.

East nodded. "I got it handled. But it took a while. Thankfully we didn't have any tenants there."

"Guests," three of my brothers said at the same time, and East just shrugged.

"Whatever."

Well, at least I knew I wasn't as grumpy as East. Though that didn't take much. I didn't know why, but then again there wasn't usually a reason for East to be an asshole. He was there when you needed him, and then he was gone like a whisper in the wind.

Apparently I needed something to eat because I was getting way too poetic.

"I have good news," I said as we took our seats around the living area and began to eat.

"You didn't ask her yet, did you?" Alexis asked. "She's going to be here soon. I thought we were going to do it together."

I held up my hand. "No, I didn't. This has to do with that, though." I sucked in a breath. "The festival has a spot open for us. We just have to go to the final place and meet with them, and then we can set up our section."

Everyone began to cheer, all talking over one another.

The South Texas Food and Booze Festival was far more eloquent than the name suggested.

Families, couples, wedding parties, event planners, and countless others went from brewery, to winery, to distillery, to just any event venue on the road trip, and ate and drank their way to bliss. The festival was written up in magazines, topped online search functions, and celebrities even came to it. It was a big thing.

And while it sounded just like a huge indulgence, it put those places on the map. It was incredibly hard to get a spot on that festival. There were countless small wineries and breweries and other event areas in the state of Texas. We were a big damn state, and you couldn't just do that road trip in a day or two. It was an event that took an entire month. People took time out of their years to make the rounds on this trip. And participating would increase the business of not only the winery itself, but Wilder Wines. We were on store shelves, and we were in wine clubs thanks to Maddie's persistence, but we were stagnant. We hadn't grown beyond that. And I knew we didn't want to become a huge company that we couldn't handle ourselves, but there was one more level we could take it, and this would help us.

"I take it Cambridge Wines didn't work out?" Evan asked with a raised brow. We'd both been on the ground floor trying to make this work while Maddie organized all around us, but nothing really felt real in that moment, not when things might be changing soon.

"Not in the slightest. Since they took over for Dodge in the past two years or so, they haven't been able to keep up with production." My lips barely resisted the urge to curl at the name Dodge and I knew my brothers all felt the same way. We'd been able to get through what old man Dodge had done in the past, as well as one of his sons, but it hadn't always easy. The fact that his other son, LJ, worked with us and was considered a friend still surprised me.

"And does that mean we can actually keep up with production?" Evan asked, a bite to his voice. I didn't blame him considering I had brought up the Dodge family. While we were friends with LJ, and worked with him, the rest of his family? No, not so much.

"No, it was because they were sloppy, and weren't professional. We're a replacement of a long-standing replacement. But we're going to kick ass. However, this does mean that I'll need to go to the brewery, the one a few stops before us, to get a handle on it and to get to know the management. I was thinking of bringing Maddie with me. I know it'll be hard for us to be gone right before we get started for our stage of the festival, but it'll be good to have her. She lights up any room that she's in, and will certainly make sure that the festival organizers understand that we're part of this for a reason."

My brothers gave each other weird looks, as my sisters-in-law kept their mouths shut.

I blinked. "Shouldn't I bring Maddie? I know we have a huge question to ask her, but I thought we could ask this as well. Not as an incentive, but this is a huge thing. She worked her ass off for this."

"Nothing's wrong," Alexis said slowly. "But it would be a road trip with the two of you. Just the two of you."

I had no idea where they were going with this. "We're friends. We'll have separate rooms. It's not a big deal. People go on work trips all the time. And Maddie is practically one of us."

Once again I caught looks and I just didn't understand it. "This is the best idea we have. We both have the ability and we'll help the Wilders. We've got this."

Elliot cleared his throat. "Okay, you do. And damn, this festival's going to be great for us. And if Maddie can't go, I'll go with you. I'm decently good with people," he said wryly.

"Maddie's going to want to go. This is her thing. But yeah, you'd be great too."

"Thank you for making me feel like I'm second best, but at least it's not seventh-best," my youngest brother Elliot said with a laugh.

I rolled my eyes, and we began talking about other plans. Someone cleared her throat from the doorway. I turned to see Maddie there, her hands clenched in front of her.

"Oh. I didn't realize it would be all of you guys. It's a Wilder board meeting."

I looked at all my family, my friends, and nodded. "Come on, take a seat. We would normally do this in the boardroom, but it's taken with the Clooney Group right now."

"I have them on a tour later today, so I'll make sure that I get them nice and happy," she said with a laugh. "So, you wanted to meet with me?"

"Stop sounding so nervous," I said. "You're fine."

She glared at me before taking her seat next to Alexis and across from me. "Thank you. Because that doesn't make me feel nervous at all."

"Why don't you take this, Elijah," Eli said, his voice low. "Since you're doing so well already."

I didn't know what everyone was on about, but I was damn excited about this, so I figured why not. "There are two big things, and they sort of go hand in hand, even though they don't. And now I'm confusing myself."

"You're confusing all of us," East growled.

I cleared my throat. "A major reason that we're even able to be considered for the festival, that we have the opportunity, is because of you."

She blinked. "What do you mean?"

"Maddie," Alexis said softly. "You work your ass off. You put all of yourself into your job, and though I came into the Wilders later, you were here. You brought these guys up to the level they needed to be."

"It's true, we'd have kind of sucked without you," Evan added.

She looked between us all, her eyes wide. "Are you guys firing me?" she asked, her voice slightly high-pitched.

"What? Of course not. We want to make you partner."

I hadn't meant to blurt that out, and as one of my brothers groaned behind me, Kendall whispered under her breath, "Good job. Smooth."

"Partner?" Maddie blurted.

I swallowed hard. "Maddie. Each of us in here owns a share of this company. But you work as hard if not harder than some of us. You put everything into this. You deserve to be a part of this. We want you to be part of this."

"Are you serious?" she asked, her voice breathy.

I met her gaze and knew that for some reason this was one of the most important things I was ever going to say.

"Maddie. You are part of our Wilder company. You always have been. Now, we'd love for you to join us. As partner. As family."

When her eyes darkened and somebody whispered behind me, I had a feeling I had just said the wrong damn thing.

Chapter Three

Maddie

My heart raced, and I wasn't quite sure I understood what they were saying. I knew all these people. They were practically family, though they weren't family. And sometimes I had to remind myself of that fact. These were my friends and my coworkers. Some of them were my bosses. But partner?

"I'm going to need you to explain that to me again. Because you want me to be partner? What does that mean?" I needed them to put it plainly so the rest of my brain could keep up.

Elijah cleared his throat, but it was Eli who spoke, and for that, I was grateful. It used to be hard to think when

Elijah was around, and while I had gotten over that, as I had grown and realized what my feelings really were, when I was thrown for a loop like this, I sometimes fell right back into old habits.

"We can go over the legalities and what it entails in detail whenever you'd like. You know we have spreadsheets and pamphlets and tons of calendars for you to look at. But the big thing is we want you to be part of this. You need a say with us. You have done so much for our company, for our family, it seems like this would be the next step. At least with your connection to us. Look over everything, ask any questions you want, take your time to decide. But we want you to be part of the Wilders."

I purposefully didn't look at Kendall or Alexis as he said that because I knew I wouldn't like what I saw in their eyes.

Pity? Knowing glances? No, I wouldn't enjoy it.

Because they knew too much. And I had an inkling that the brothers did too. The only person that had never honestly realized that I thought I had been in love with Elijah was Elijah himself. And perhaps that should have told me something. It would have saved me a lot of pain and angst.

I'd stood on that hilltop next to him while he was grieving, screaming at the world for daring to take Joy. I had been right next to him when he vowed he would never love again. That no matter what came at him, Joy was it. Nobody else would be the person for him, and nobody else would pull him towards that deep emotion that had carved out a section of his soul.

I had already begun to bury those emotions when I figured out that he and Joy were truly perfect for each other. And during that time, Joy and I had become friends. I had truly liked being with her, and I had always hoped that she never knew my feelings toward Elijah. Because that had never been on her, I would have survived watching them marry and have children and be happy. I would have found a way.

But knowing that Elijah was never going to fall in love again, that was what had broken the final straw and what had given me the courage to finally move on. Something I had needed to do long before then.

"I don't know what to say."

"Say yes," Elliot said, and East grunted while Evan just rolled his eyes silently.

"Take your time," Everett put in. "It's a big thing."

Elijah spoke next, walking towards me. He stopped at least a foot away, but I swore I could feel the heat of him. Or perhaps that was me going faint from everything coming at me at once.

"We'd love for you to be part of this. You've earned it. You took a chance on us when we were afraid we were going to fuck everything up."

"Language," Alexis teased.

I cringed. "I think I need a lot of time to think. And to go over everything. But I'm truly grateful."

I ignored the guilt sliding through me because there was another reason I was so off-kilter. But I didn't know if it was time to tell them.

"Good. Think about it. However, I do have good news," Elijah said, and the brothers beamed.

I stiffened, my pulse racing. "What is it?" I asked.

"We got the festival."

I broke out into a grin and threw my arms around Elijah's neck. He hugged me back as I cheered and realized that the others hadn't clapped with me or made any movement. Of course, they hadn't. They knew about the festival. They had probably already spoken about it, and here I was, throwing my arms around Elijah and climbing over the man who was nearly my boss but not quite.

I cleared my throat and slid off him. He squeezed my hips and winked.

I knew that was just because he thought I was cute or something from being so excited. It wasn't sexual or heated in any way. But my damn libido did not understand. Neither did my heart.

Fuck my heart. I was tired of letting it lead me in directions that were just going to hurt me in the end. It was just an old wound, an echo of what I had once wanted. I didn't need to deal with that again. I needed to get over myself.

Because the festival was fucking important. And my former emotional attachment and angst towards Elijah Wilder weren't.

And once I got that through my head, I would be a bigger person. A better person.

Or at least a more mentally stable person. Whatever.

"Anyway," I said, and I knew my face had to be red, "We did it!" A pause. "You did it."

"You were right the first time. *We* did it. We got the festival. We'll have more details soon, hopefully not in a reply-all email like before," he said wryly, and I laughed.

The others gave us odd looks, and I realized that they hadn't been included on the emails. It was odd to think that Elijah and I had that thing that was just for us. No, I needed to stop thinking like that. I was just a little scatterbrained.

"Do we know when yet?"

"We'll be the second to last stop on the festival, which does mean that there'll need to be Wilder representation at one of the founding events."

"You're going to go, right? You'd be the best at it. Especially for Wilder Wines."

"That's exactly what I said about you," Elijah said, and I blinked. I looked around at the others. Sometimes it was hard to remember that these were all his family members, and yet they had been in the room and hadn't said anything while Elijah and I were talking.

"You have to go," Alexis said softly. "This will be great for you."

"Oh. Well. Instead of Elijah? I know you just offered me partner, but don't you think a Wilder should be there?"

"*We* would go, the two of us," Elijah said, as if that wasn't out of the ordinary. And of course, it shouldn't be, but it was.

Evan cleared his throat. "I would go, but I can't schmooze like you guys can."

"It's not schmoozing, it's being nice," I teased.

Kendall just grinned and looked at her husband. "She's got you."

"True. But while I know the wine, you guys know the business more. And I know you can sell anything. And, well, the festival's your baby."

"Oh. I mean..." I had been trying to get into this festival since before the Wilders even owned the company. When I worked for the original winery, I had done my best to try to keep the company afloat. We had done well, but we did better as Wilders. And each year I tried to get on the circuit, but there either hadn't been space, or the Dodges hurt our chances. I knew that the Wilders' friend's brewery was on the circuit every other year, because that's how he liked it. There was a lot of stress and time and money that went into providing a stop of the festival, but it would be worth it in the end. Especially because I knew the Wilders wanted to make this a future. For their family, and for their legacy.

And they wanted me to be part of it. Not just with this trip and this festival itself, but by becoming a bigger component of the company. I wasn't even sure I could comprehend exactly what all of that meant or what I was supposed to say, so I didn't think about that yet. I couldn't. Not if I needed to function.

But I could think about the trip.

"A road trip. I can do that. I want to make sure we kick ass at this."

Elijah grinned. "I knew you would."

There was something about him. He just looked happier. Or maybe I was losing my mind.

Maybe I was seeing things that weren't really there.

"We'll go over all the details, but you think about the news, and then we'll work on this road trip. It'll be fun." He tapped me on the shoulder as if I was one of the guys, and I refused to let myself deflate. Because we had all worked hard for this moment, I wasn't going to fail.

I also knew that they needed to have the whole story.

They started to talk about other things and I took notes, knowing that even if I stayed in this role, and I didn't move up, and I didn't make changes, I was still part of this process.

There was a big wedding coming up, one that was taking a lot more effort than they anticipated because of familial issues, but Alexis was handling it like a dream. East was dealing with some maintenance issues that came with owning property in South Texas in the heat during a drought. And things just kept getting added to the list, and I nodded, adding my input when I could. But before we broke up, I needed to say something, because they needed to know the whole story.

And frankly, I was terrible at keeping secrets. I hadn't kept one well enough, and look where it got me.

I cleared my throat as the conversation wound down, and I knew the meeting would be over soon. "Before you go, I have something to say."

Everyone stared at me, and I hated this. While I was fine being the center of attention in some circumstances, when I was about to drop a bomb wasn't one of them.

"First, thank you for everything. For believing in me, for the offer. And I'm going to go over everything and will have questions I promise you. But you need to know everything."

The room suddenly shifted, people straightening, staring at me. I swallowed hard and continued, bracing myself.

"Ivy Wines approached me with a job offer, as the replacement for their operations director for the winery. I haven't said yes, and I haven't fully even investigated it. They approached me. I didn't approach them. But I've been thinking about it. And it's been killing me not to say anything. But I thought you should know."

You could have heard a pin drop as the brothers stared at me, each with identical faces. No expression, as if they weren't sure what they were supposed to feel or say in this situation, even Elijah. And usually I could read him, even when he did his best to mask his emotions.

It was Alexis who spoke first. "That would be an amazing opportunity for you. I know you've been in your role here for a while now, and I know growth is something that we all want. So that would be amazing for you."

I looked at her then and rolled my eyes. "And it would suck because it's over three hours away, and I'd be leaving my friends and family and everything that I built here. But you're right, it's not that I'm stagnant here, but I want to learn, and I want to push myself. And pushing myself with this festival and trying to get it for so many years has been an amazing thing for us. It is what I've wanted for the Wilders. I hadn't even thought about becoming partner with you guys at all. It never even occurred to me that it was possible. So while I haven't said anything to Ivy yet, I wanted you to know it's out there. And I'm not trying to put it out there as a negotiation tactic or anything. I just want to be open. Because I hate secrets, and I hate feeling like I'm going in a thousand different directions."

I would have said more, but East held up his hand. Quiet East who only growled when he felt like it sometimes.

"You need to do what's best for you. I like Ivy Wines. Not as much as I like ours," he said as Evan glared. "But you're right. We all work well together because it's what we've clung to when we had no idea what we needed to do. But even Everett over here doesn't work on location every week. We're changing how we work. So thanks for letting us know. We're not going to pressure you, although we Wilders do pressure just by being in a room."

"Was that a joke?" Elliot asked, his hand over his

heart. "East just made a joke. Okay, somebody get me wine. This is just too much, even for the beginning of the day."

That broke the tension and I laughed, shaking my head. "I don't know what I'm going to do. I need facts. You know I do. And while sometimes I lead with emotion, right now, I just need to work. So, let's plan for the road trip because I'm not going anywhere anytime soon. You got me?"

Elijah met my gaze, and once again, I couldn't read him. "Of course. We're going to do this, and then we'll figure out what's next. It's what we always do."

And with that, the meeting broke up, and I smiled and was grateful when my phone rang.

"It's a club. I've got to go."

The girls gave me a look, and I knew I would have to talk about it soon. But not right then. Thankfully.

———

By the time I finished the call, everyone had spread out to get on with the rest of their day, and I was grateful. I had been afraid to bring up Ivy Wines with them, but I hated hiding it. I had been truthful. I hadn't approached them. But the job offer was lucrative, and it sparked something. It was something new and shiny and would push me at levels I wasn't ready for. But maybe I could be. And I wanted a challenge.

I went towards my office, knowing that Elijah and I needed to plan our trip, but that wasn't something I wanted to think about. Being alone in a car with Elijah for days, having to pretend that I wasn't possibly leaving the company, or joining it in a new way, or forgetting the fact that I used to love him. Oh great. That wasn't going to be difficult at all.

I turned the corner, smacked into a hard chest, and looked up at a very familiar face.

Nathaniel looked down at me, smiling softly. "Hey, babe."

There was something in that, something I couldn't quite interpret, or perhaps it was just because I was in my head.

"I didn't know you were here. Why didn't you tell me you were here?"

He leaned down and brushed a casual kiss to my cheek, but not to my lips. What was wrong? He didn't tend to tell me everything, in fact, I didn't even know when his next gig was after the wedding here. I needed to ask him, but then when I did, he rarely told me. We just didn't mesh all the time and I used to be fine with that. I thought it was all I needed. He didn't know everything about me and my day. We rarely talked. And if I were honest with myself...we rarely did much of anything else either.

And it just occurred to me, not once did I think about telling Nathaniel about the job from Ivy, or being offered partner. Or even the road trip. It didn't occur to me to tell the man I was dating about these huge life changes for me.

And that was wrong. Because if it was so casual in my mind that I didn't even have an inkling to tell him big parts of my life—things I just had to spill to the Wilders because I couldn't hold back—I didn't need this.

He looked at me then and let out a rough chuckle that twisted deep inside. It was familiar in that it wasn't cruel, but inevitable. "I see it in your eyes."

I blinked. "See what?"

"This isn't working, Maddie. You know it as well as I do. It's not that you aren't great. Because you are."

I winced at the words, wondering how they could sound so blameless and full of blame at the same time. "Oh, that's a great line to hear."

"You're thinking it too. We are damn good at sex, and we have fun when we date, but you're not into it, Maddie. I think I know why, but maybe I don't. But it's fine. I think it'd be better off if we just remain friends. Or I can be that dashing guy at the mic when I'm singing at a wedding, and you laugh and maybe dance with me one time or another on the dance floor. But you're not in love with me, and I don't think you're ever going to be."

"Nathaniel. I don't...this isn't what I wanted to say..." I began, but he shook his head.

"I don't think I could ever love you, Maddie. And I know that probably sucks to hear, but I think it's just because we're comfortable. And I want that love that breaks your heart and tears at you so hard that you write lyrics for it and make the best rock ballad ever. And we're not those people for each other. We're good for comfort and for a scheduled routine. But, I don't know, I don't want to be your second best or fourth best. And I don't even know if I have a first best. Or is it just best? See? You have me all in my head."

I swallowed hard. "Nathaniel, I'm sorry. And I hate the fact that you're right. I don't love you and the fact that you said you could never love me should be breaking me right now. Only it's not and that probably means you're much stronger than I am in saying that first." I only felt relief. And that was wrong.

He leaned down and brushed his lips across mine, a soft caress that felt like a goodbye, but didn't bring me to tears. It didn't ache or tear at my soul.

When he pulled away, I knew that we were done. I wouldn't feel that again, not with him, and maybe not with anyone. And wasn't that just the epitome of lost?

"Find that spark, Maddie. You deserve it. Now, I am going to have some wine. And I hear there's a decent bottle around here, too."

"I think I can help with that."

Someone cleared his throat, and I looked back to see Jay standing there as he waved Nathaniel through. "Come on. I'll give you a tour. I know a decent wine or two to help with that."

He winked, and I was grateful that it was Jay who had

witnessed my humiliation and not a Wilder. I wasn't quite sure I could deal with the ups and downs of everything that had just happened in the face of a Wilder.

I looked down at my phone and was grateful for the time, because instead of only dealing with the fact that I had just broken up with my boyfriend—or possibly had gotten dumped—at my place of work, I had also just gotten a monumental job offer, and I ignored it all. Instead, I got in my car, glad it was the end of my day.

I had to get ready for my trip and pretend that I knew what I was doing. Because frankly, I didn't.

Not even a little.

I pulled into my driveway, my mind going in a thousand different directions as I tried to keep up with the fact that I didn't know what I should do.

Should I stay with the Wilders? I had the money to buy in, I thought. I'd glanced over the paperwork during my workday, though I still needed to study it more, and with a lawyer. But I could buy in reasonably. I could have my hands deep in the process and make us grow. It was something I didn't know could ever be on my plate, but I loved the thought. It could be amazing. I just didn't know.

And then there was Ivy Wines, which was a whole new opportunity. It would be basically Elijah's job, something I hadn't done before but felt confident I could do.

All of this at once, including the festival that we would have to plan at our place, as well as the road trip. I just needed to go home, make a list, take a bath, and have a glass of wine. Because wine fixed anything.

I got out of my car and waved at Martha next door.

Martha was a widow who had lived in her house for as long as I could remember. She was sweet and baked amazing snickerdoodles. She also loved baking fruit pies and did her best to teach me, though I wasn't the greatest at pastry. Her kids had moved far away with their own families, but came out to visit her often.

"Did you have a good day at work, darling?"

I smiled, warmth sliding through me at her words. We might not be related by blood, but she felt like a kind aunt who always cared about my day.

"I did. A long day but a good one. I'm going on a trip soon, though. I'll give you the details so you don't worry when you don't see me. How was your day?"

"Oh, I hope you have fun with your young man. And my day was pleasant as always, darling."

She'd never met Nathaniel. In fact, she'd never met any of the men I'd dated. The only man she'd met was Elijah, but to dissuade her of that notion was like pushing a boulder up a hill. It wasn't happening.

"I'm glad you had a good day." Martha had some health issues and was sometimes forgetful but was always very sweet. She waved at me and went back to her knitting, staring at the sunset that always brought hope to my heart. There was nothing like a Texas sunset. At least to this Texan girl.

I walked inside, grateful for the time to think, and hoped that I knew what I was doing.

I had a few decisions to make, but first, I needed to come up with a plan on how exactly to deal with the road trip with Elijah.

And ask myself why that was first on my list.

Chapter Four

Elijah

Why did I feel as if I were wrapped in a cocoon of awkwardness and dunked in a vat of what the fuck?

I had been in a car with Maddie before, of course. This wasn't the first time we had ridden together for any period of time, but it felt different for some reason. As if this was a first time, as if I was supposed to be saying something other than what I was.

We had at least a four-and-a-half-hour drive to the place where our visiting part of the festival would occur. Depending on traffic, construction, and other humans, it could take longer.

I was the one driving this time, and I tended to go around ten miles over the speed limit. I liked driving in the middle lane, so people who wanted to go eighty or ninety or faster—the insane individuals—could. And then I could go around the tractors, the tourists, and the people who wanted to go fifty-five in a seventy-five.

"I will never understand South Texas drivers," I mumbled.

I hadn't realized that I had said the words out loud until Maddie snorted.

"Just South Texas drivers? Or *all* Texas drivers?"

I tapped my fingers against the steering wheel and pointed to the road. "Do you notice that the further north we get on I-35, the faster we're going?"

"Perhaps it's because the speed limit's increasing?"

I shook my head and turned on my blinker, going around an SUV that happened to be illegally lifted for some reason, going sixty-five miles an hour in the center lane.

"No, it's still seventy-five miles an hour like it was in the Forum corridor where we live. No, it's because where we live, people think that speed limits are just that. A limit. So they take their Sunday drive on every day of the week and never go near the upper limit."

"You're still mad about that truck going thirty-five miles an hour, aren't you?"

I held up my hand, that familiar rage sliding through me. "Thirty-five miles an hour in a fifty! There was a line of at least thirty cars behind that man, and he just lazily puttered along. I'm pretty sure the horse next to us was going faster."

"In the pasture? No, I don't think that's possible," she singsonged.

She had her tablet in her hands while going over work things. We had enough time to talk over our festival plans, as well as how we were going to approach this meeting. But right then, talking about traffic sounded a little easier. Or perhaps I just needed to get it out.

"Seriously though, I do not understand it. They just take their time. Even on the highway when it's seventy-five fucking miles an hour, they go fifty-five. And they are all in the middle and right lanes. Nobody gets over at the on-ramps, so people bottleneck getting on the highway. The left lane is full of people wanting to go ninety but stuck behind people going the speed limit because they're passing the people going forty. And the access roads are even worse because they're wondering when they're supposed to turn, so they go twenty-five in a forty-five."

"Then there are those people that like to go ninety on both," Maddie added, and I grinned.

"That's not me, but sometimes I want to. It's why I'm glad that this baby has the big engine." I patted the dashboard. "Although my next car's going to be electric. We're getting the infrastructure now. It's time."

She leaned toward me, our conversation feeling like it used to. Simple and easy. "I was looking at one, and there's a charging station in between my house and the Wilder property. It could work."

"I know many people have charging stations in their homes, too."

"Or at least the adapters. I'm looking into it. It's on my long list to research. You know, the Wilders should invest in one."

I smiled. "It's on the list. East wants to go over the mechanics of it so he understands it, rather than us just plugging in a car and accidentally shutting down the entire complex."

"I don't think that's how it works."

"But I don't know how it works. I need to do research. We already have solar panels on most of the buildings that we can, and East is wondering if we should put a whole new section in the pasture area."

"That section that no one ever goes to, and nothing grows because they over-farmed it before it was turned into a venue?"

"Exactly. It's just sitting there collecting snakes and other creatures. I don't know, East has ideas, and maybe he can turn it into a bigger garden for Kendall."

"The garden on the property is getting quite small for the amount of farm-to-table she's using." She paused. "Don't use the phrase farm-to-table in front of her. She gets a little snippy about it."

I laughed. "It's because everybody and their mother used farm-to-table, and now it's overused and ridiculous."

"Pretty much, so I just let her have what she wants."

This felt good. The two of us talking. Only I didn't want to say that. I didn't want to make things more awkward. They were already awkward. Because we hadn't talked about the fact that we had offered her partner. I wasn't sure she was going to take it. I was terrified we were about to lose the best thing that had ever happened to the Wilder Resort. She was everything to us. She had been a touchstone for our company and our family, and now I didn't know what would happen next, and I hated that. I hated that we might lose her.

That I might lose her.

I frowned, wondering where that thought came from. It didn't make much sense. Not when this was Maddie. My friend. She had been there through everything with us. I didn't know why I was acting like this.

"I got your last email, by the way," she added, laughter in her tone.

"I have no idea what you're talking about."

I knew what she was talking about. Ever since the debacle with the festival organizer's email, the two of us had been adding extra emails to our day. Yes, we normally emailed, texted, and messaged one another countless times a day for work and meeting up, but these were different.

We were joking, not talking about anything too serious, but it was just Maddie and me.

Had I been flirting with her? No. That would be wrong.

No, she didn't work for me, she worked with me, but still, I shouldn't.

Especially because, well, she was family. Wasn't she? I liked her.

A little too much.

But that didn't matter because she might be leaving, and I knew that she thought of us Wilders like her brothers.

So I was never going to do anything beyond an email.

My phone buzzed and I looked down at it. Maddie tapped me on the elbow and took the phone from the holder.

"Eyes on the road. I'm not in the mood to get in a car accident because you're not paying attention."

We both froze as she said it, that familiar icy feeling sliding over me.

"I'm sorry. I'm so sorry."

I cleared my throat. "It's okay. I'm okay."

And I wasn't lying to myself either. I wasn't lying to her. That surprised me more than anything.

Out of the corner of my eye, I saw her studying me. I hoped she understood I wasn't lying.

She kept staring at me before she cleared her throat and finally looked down at the phone.

She was silent for so long that I was afraid I had once again said something wrong.

"What is it?"

"It's, um, it's Joy's parents."

My hands tightened on the steering wheel and I passed another slow car.

"What do they say?"

"They were just wondering when you would be back in town for your dinner."

I sighed. "Will you tell them I'm driving and I will get back to them soon? And that it's you texting?"

She turned to me then, and I couldn't help but look at her for a moment before putting my eyes back on the road.

"You want them to know I have your phone?"

The way she said it made me feel like I was doing something wrong, but I wasn't. Not with Maddie.

"Yes. They know you. They like you. And they know I'm going on this trip with you. It would make sense."

She let out a breath that sounded a little relieved, though I didn't know why she would be nervous, before she texted back.

"They say good luck, kick butt, and they'll talk to you soon."

She cleared her throat and set the phone down.

"I didn't know you spoke with them often."

My hands tapped on the steering wheel as I moved in my seat, oddly uncomfortable. "Not daily or anything. But enough. We were friends. I'm never going to be their son-in-law, and they don't think of me as their son. At least, I don't think so. I don't think of them as my parents. But it's an odd sense of figuring out who we are and what we lost together. They have other children, Joy's siblings. They love them very much and do their best to make sure that they are present in their lives and their grandchildren's lives. I might be a reminder of Joy, but I'm not the only one. I think they just want to make sure that Joy is remembered, but it's not the only thing we have in our lives."

I hadn't meant to get so deep, to speak so much, but Maddie was silent for a long time.

"It's nice that you have each other. To heal with one another, or to just live these new parts of your lives. I'm not sure I would ever be able to do that."

"I hope you never have to deal with anything that gets you there."

Once again, she was silent for long enough that I wasn't sure what to say.

"When we get back, are you ever going to bring Nathaniel to one of our Wilder company events?"

I had no idea why I was asking that. It made no sense. I didn't want to know about her and Nathaniel. It was crossing some line. Though I didn't know exactly what it was.

"Nathaniel and I aren't together anymore."

My car beeped as I accidentally moved too close to the center lane, and Maddie braced herself.

"Elijah. Car. Big car."

"Sorry, you surprised me. When did that happen?"

"Yesterday. It's fine. I guess I should be single for a while. I've tried dating, but it's too difficult. Especially with everything going on."

"What's going on?"

She gave me a weird look as I continued to drive.

"So it didn't work out with those other two guys, either? Jackson or Samuel?"

"I can't believe you even remember their names."

"Of course, I remember, Maddie. You were dating them. I'm not going to forget that."

She stared at me for long enough that I knew I had indeed said the wrong thing. Or maybe just a damn weird thing.

"Are you really leaving?" I asked as I pulled off at our exit, grateful we were getting close to the brewery. I hadn't meant to say that, to even ask, but there was no going back now.

"I might. I need new challenges. I need something. I feel like I've gone as far as I can here. Which sounds so ungrateful. Here we are, going to this festival that we've worked so hard for, to bring our company into, and it's just that. It's our company. But I feel like I'm treading water. And I don't like that."

"We can challenge you," I blurted.

I didn't want her to leave. I wanted Maddie to stay. But that was for purely selfish reasons, wasn't it? Selfish reasons for the company.

Only the company.

"You always do," she mumbled.

The GPS began to speak again, cutting her off, and I was grateful. I didn't want to know what she wanted to say because I didn't know her answer. Where she would go.

We pulled into the new brewery inn that was like our friend Roy's, down near us. We were in North Texas now, and this place was huge. It was built by the same owner of a winery already on the tour, so they had gotten their slot. Apparently, the owner would alternate his two businesses every other year. It was a good deal, and as I stared at the vast expanse of the inn, the brewery building, and all the activities that they had planned, I knew we had a lot to do.

I turned off the car and looked at Maddie, taking a deep breath.

"We're here. Let's learn. And wine and dine and make sure that they know we're going to kick ass even more."

She smiled then, but it was a little too bright, a little too forced.

"Maddie. We want you. We want you to stay."

She shook her head. "Okay. I know. But let's not talk about that now. We have other things to do."

"Okay. Let's go kick ass."

"Of course, we will. What else would we do?"

She got out of the car, leaving me there for a moment, trying to catch my breath.

What the hell was wrong with me?

This was Maddie.

Just Maddie.

And yet there was nothing *just* about her. And that was what scared me.

Chapter Five

Maddie

The competitive part of me wanted to hate this place. I wanted the Wilder Retreat and Winery to be the best. To be the number one place on the circuit, which everybody talked about and put everyone else to shame.

I would do my best to make that happen. For now, I just smiled as I stood at the Dustin Cousins Brewery.

The Dustin Cousins Brewery had another name, one a little more eloquent and classier. Still, the Dustin cousins themselves had become such an entertaining group, along with their families, that they'd ended up going by their nickname for most things. They were still the Center

Creek Brewery, and all of their labels, beers, ciders, and other items were denoted as such, but the Dustin cousins were the ones that people thought of.

The place was gorgeous, with sprawling grounds fit for families, newlyweds, work retreats, and everything the Wilders did.

They, like our friend Roy, were focused on beer. And though I wasn't a huge beer drinker, I had already fallen in love with the blondes and their cider. Now, most breweries didn't also have a cidery, that was a whole other thing, but they paired with a local company. They even shipped in apples from the Northeast to make blends. I didn't know how it worked or exactly what made the perfect cider or blonde, but I had learned a bit on the tour and planned to do my own research. Mostly because I was enjoying myself.

I hadn't thought I would enjoy myself, not after the awkward and oddly heated conversations with Elijah in the car. I hadn't meant to say anything. I didn't know why things were suddenly so weird with him.

No, I *did* know why things were weird, but I didn't want them to be weird, and that was what bothered me.

I was doing my best not to take things too far or think about the past, yet all I was doing these days was thinking about Elijah.

I should be heartbroken over the fact that I was just dumped—despite the fact it had been far too long since I'd been with Nathaniel. I felt guilty that I had an offer from

Ivy Wines, yet elated that they thought I was worth pursuing. They were offering me a shit ton of money. Yes, I would have to start over in a new place in Texas. I would be competing with the Wilders, although Ivy Wines didn't have the same retreat and inn area that the Wilders did. But the wines would be sitting next to each other on the shelves, and part of me would be blended into each of those wines, but I would still be competing with my past.

That could be the problem. Competing with the path I had traveled, the stones that had paved that journey, and now I wanted to make my own path. Or whatever other metaphor fit.

I needed a new home, a new adventure.

And yet, part of me could only think about coming home. To find that place where everything just made sense.

The Wilders were offering me a partnership. A stake in who they were, beyond being their employee. I would be working alongside Elijah day in and day out, even more than I already was, and we would be equals. And I hated myself for wanting that. For wanting one more obstacle out of the way between us.

And yet, the largest obstacle was him. Because Elijah didn't want me. He didn't want the happiness and passion that came from a relationship. He had already had that. I didn't want to be his second choice. His second best.

He had loved and lost his first choice. His happy ever after.

I would be his second chance, a chance and choice he didn't even want. And it wasn't even me. He said that he did not want it at all. So I would be competing with a ghost. And I already did that daily as it was. Maybe I should move on. And leave. Maybe it would make things easier.

I just wanted things to be easier.

"Your glass is empty, and there's a sad smile on your face. While I can certainly fix one, maybe I can try the other," a deep voice said from beside me.

I turned and put on my best fake worker smile as Clint Dustin of the Dustin cousins came forward. He was tall, with broad shoulders, a narrow waist, and was gorgeous hell. He was also very single.

Most of the other cousins were already married off, but he wasn't. The only reason I knew that was because I had gone to the restroom earlier and heard some other women mention it. He was the talk of the town, because most of the people visiting each of these festival locations as other brewery, cidery, and winery owners were married. Or at least deeply entwined, so finding single people on this type of trip was rare.

I was one of the oddly many single women in attendance, because we were all support staff. I loved the fact that there were so many women in my position, since for some reason this was usually a very male-driven area.

But Elijah and Clint were among the very few single men here.

And from the way everyone kept letting their gazes prowl over the two men, every single *single* woman here knew it. I didn't like the way their gazes raked over them, the way it looked as if Elijah and Clint were both appetizers before the delicious food part of the festival began.

And I didn't like the fact that Clint was looking at me just now as if he wanted to pry into my mind and see what made me tick. Because he also had that look in his eyes. That look that hinted of something other than work.

Well, damn it. A woman knew when she was being hit on, even if he hadn't said the words. And I had no idea what to think about that.

"Your blonde was amazing. Perfectly light, and yet with a depth that surprised me."

"That's our goal. Sometimes you don't need all those heavy beers and IPAs after a long day. Sometimes you just want something a little refreshing. Different."

Well, that wasn't subtle at all.

He groaned as he held out the glass.

"I wasn't trying to sound like a lecher just then, but it happened. I'm sorry. Hello, I'm Clint Dustin. How are you?"

I laughed. I couldn't help it. "I'm just fine. I'm Maddie Swift."

"I know. I saw you coming in with Elijah. I've heard good things about you."

I raised a brow. "Really?"

"Beer and wine aren't always in the same circles, hell,

they're not even allowed to be sold in the same stores in some states."

"Blue laws are fun."

"We have our own things, but yes. We can be side by side here."

I raised a brow.

"They just are so easy sometimes. I'm sorry. I promise I'll stop putting on the moves. Even accidentally."

"See, that also sounded like a line. A little too smooth." I sipped my beer, the refreshing taste sliding over my tongue.

"But what I meant to say was, I have heard of you. Your stats with the wine clubs with Wilder Wines are becoming legendary."

I snorted and nearly spilled my beer. "Really? That's what you're going with?"

"It's the truth. You know what you're doing. It's why Ivy Wines wants you."

This time I did slosh some of the beer over the side.

"Excuse me?"

He held out his hand.

"I'm sorry. I didn't mean to stress you out. I'm friends with the owner of Ivy Wines, and while I was looking to fill a similar position, they mentioned who they were looking at. While your job offer isn't exactly confidential, it was just mentioned in passing." He paused as I tried to consider the ramifications of that. "Do the Wilders know?"

"I don't know if that's exactly your business," I said, frowning.

"You're right. It's not. But I'm just curious."

"They know. And they know I'm still thinking about it. I'm not ready to make any decisions."

"Well, that's good. You need to make them work for it. After all, you worked your ass off for them, and the company before that."

"You seem to know a lot about me, and I don't know too much about you."

"How much do you want to know about me?" he asked, his voice going low.

"Dustin, it's good to see you," a deep voice said beside me as Elijah walked up. He gently touched his shoulder to mine as he moved past, and I swallowed hard. I was wearing stilettos, and he was still taller than me, but the motion nearly knocked me over.

Clint didn't miss the touch and frowned for an instant before he smiled again.

"I've been monopolizing your taster here."

"Maddie's the best manager we have."

I rolled my eyes at that. "I'm the only manager you have. But thanks for that," I said dryly.

"You know your worth. So do we. Seriously though, Dustin, this place is great. I liked coming here before, and you guys have only gotten better."

Clint relaxed at that, leaning back on his heels. "We try. Roy gives us competition, but only the good kind."

"That's what we like to hear. He's a good man, and so are you, I hear."

There was a touch of something in that tone I couldn't understand, but then again, I couldn't really keep up. Because we weren't here to act territorial. We needed to kick ass at this festival. And I knew we were going to. This tour would bring many new people to our business and only elevate it.

And the fact that I kept calling it *our* business meant that I felt that I was one of the Wilders.

Even though here we were, talking about me possibly leaving, and I didn't know what I wanted. And I hated being wishy-washy. I was not that person. I made decisions, and I stuck to it. Like how I told myself I wouldn't love Elijah.

I needed to stop overthinking.

The guys had kept talking while I was lost in thought, before Clint looked down at his phone.

"If you'll excuse me, my cousin needs me for something. I know you guys are going to understand this soon, but this whole festival thing is exhausting. Good, but exhausting."

"You guys are doing a great job."

"And I bet you want to do better. I see that glint in your eyes. Game on."

He winked before he said goodbye, and Elijah cleared his throat. "That was interesting."

I sipped more of my beer. "Oh really? What?"

He stared at me and shook his head. "Nothing, I guess. Maybe I'm just seeing things."

There was a lot of that going around recently.

"Do you have any ideas for our stop?"

"Tons, and I bet you do too. This place is fantastic, though. I know we're going to have to fight to keep our spot, to elevate it, but we can. Especially with you with us."

"Elijah," I began, and he shook his head.

"I'm going to go mingle. You should too. You're great at it."

He pushed my hair from my face before he left, and I was left wondering why he had done that.

I hated that he touched me. Gently, the way a friend would, the way that someone would when you had been near each other for so long that it was second nature.

Elijah moved over to a group of festival-goers, and women flocked to him. They flirted, fluttered their eyelashes, and put their hands on his arms as they spoke. Elijah, a strong man who knew what he wanted, let them and flirted right back. At least flirted in a friendly manner. Perhaps he didn't even know he was doing it.

And that dragon inside me, that little jealous bitch, clawed at me. I hated it.

And while I knew I needed to be part of this, this festival, and to push the Wilders to the stratosphere, this possibly needed to be my last time.

Because I thought I was over him, but I wasn't. So fuck

it. I wasn't going to whine. I wasn't going to hate myself. But I wasn't going to put myself in this position anymore.

I needed to move on. And even though I knew I could do amazing things as a partner, I could be challenged elsewhere.

I loved him. I wanted him. And that was a damn problem.

I had lied to myself for so long, and now it was time to change my situation.

To take care of myself.

Even if it broke me.

Chapter Six

Elijah

I began to pack up everything in the car, frowning as I looked at my weather app on my phone.

"We're going to be hitting storms on our way back."

I looked over at Maddie, wondering why she was so quiet this morning. Something had happened the night before. And I didn't know what it was. She was quieter and pulled away from me. Or maybe I was seeing things.

"It's this time of year in Texas. Storms are inevitable. But we'll be okay."

I snorted and closed the trunk of the SUV. "You say that as if you're going to will it to happen."

She looked at me, a single brow raised. She looked like her old self for just a minute before her face went blank again.

"If I have to will it to happen, I will. We have a lot of things to do when we get back, and we need to get started."

"We're taking turns driving, like you wanted, so whoever's in the passenger seat can work. We'll talk about things. See what happens."

"Sure. We can do that."

I frowned at her. "What's wrong, Maddie?"

She was quiet for so long that I feared I had said the wrong thing again. I was too damn good about saying the wrong thing.

"Nothing is wrong. Let's just get in the car," she said after a minute.

We got on the road quickly and went over everything we'd learned throughout the weekend.

"I do like that brewery. They have a lot to offer. Though I believe our retreat is better, just because I'm biased."

"So, you liked the brewery? Or Clint?"

I hadn't meant to ask that, and I could have bitten off my tongue.

She paused and looked at me with wide eyes. "Are you serious right now?"

"Not really. Forget I said that."

"Did you think that I only like that brewery because you think that I'm attracted to Clint Dustin?"

"Like I said, forget about everything. I had a long night. I'm tired."

All excuses.

"Would that be because you were up all night with Barbara? Or was it Clarice? Or Claire? Or Evie? Or Evelyn? Or Jessica? Or the countless other women that were fawning all over you for the entire event?"

My hands gripped the steering wheel a little tighter, and I glared at her before changing lanes. "You know all of their names?"

"I take it you don't. Well, that's surprising. Coming from you."

"I vaguely remember their names as I was introduced to them, but I wasn't particularly interested in any of them."

No, I was particularly interested in someone else, someone that I knew was very bad for me.

And that was the crux of it, wasn't it? Because I wasn't supposed to feel this attraction to anyone else. Especially not Maddie. Dammit. Why was I even thinking of her? Yes, we were speaking, and we were in the same damn car, but I wasn't supposed to think of her as someone I was attracted to. This was fucking *Maddie*. What was wrong with me?

"You know what, this conversation is perilously close to something that we do not need to talk about."

"Oh, we have moved way past that." I paused, trying to collect myself. I never thought about Maddie like this. Or rather, I did my best not to. When we first met, there was an attraction there. Of course, there had been. She was gorgeous, brilliant, and just a damn good person. Every time I was near her, it was hard for me to think. All I had done was trip over myself, trying to not act like I felt anything around her. And I realized that there was never going to be anything. And that there shouldn't be, considering she worked with me. So I buried those feelings. Then I had found Joy. And Joy wasn't here anymore, and Maddie might not be either soon.

And at that sobering thought, I cleared my throat.

"I liked the brewery. They did a fantastic job. All of the Dustins. I'm sorry."

"No, I'm sorry. We both crossed the line."

Thunder cracked, and I frowned as I stared at the large storm we were heading into.

"Do me a favor? Will you check the weather app and see if we're under any warnings? I don't like the look of that. Especially those clouds. They look a little too funnel-like."

"Shit. You're right. Okay, we're in a tornado watch. No, that's a warning. Damn it. I can't really tell. The signal isn't great out here."

I looked off into the distance and swore, my pulse racing at a sight I'd seen a few times before. Fuck.

"I'm going to need you to be calm and gently look over to the right a bit while I get off the highway and go east."

Maddie froze, and I watched her turn slightly towards the west before she cursed under her breath.

"Well. That's a circling set of clouds that could be a funnel at some point. Oh my God. And I sound far calmer than I feel because, holy fucking shit. It's very far in the distance, and I think it's moving away, but well, let's get off the road. I don't need to have cows spinning around us."

"If my memory serves, it was just a single cow in that movie."

"And while we're not in a truck, we are in a red SUV. So now I'm picturing two dueling tornadoes and us under a bridge. But it never works out like that in real life."

"No, a single belt isn't going to keep us alive with F5 storms above us."

"Oh, the magic of television. I'm going to start talking very quickly as we get away from this. *Because that's a damn almost-tornado.*"

"You've seen them before," I said as I tried to sound calm, getting off the highway.

"Well, yes. But we're not technically in Tornado Alley. It's not like I really see them often."

I looked out the rearview mirror and sighed. "It's dissipated. We're fine."

For now. Though I didn't say that aloud.

She let out a relieved breath of her own and shook her

head. "The storm is getting worse. We're going straight into it. We either turn back, or we find somewhere to stay for now." She kept scrolling on her phone as the rain intensified, the windshield wipers going as fast as they could, and not doing much. When the hail began, I cursed again and took another exit, grateful that I saw a hotel sign in the distance.

"Hopefully, there are vacancies because we're staying here tonight." I clenched the steering wheel tight as the roads grew slick and the rain pounded loudly enough it was hard to think.

"The weather apps are saying that it's just going to get worse and that it's moving so slow that flooding is going to be a problem. And the direction we're going is all flash flood area. Crap. When I looked earlier, it wasn't this bad."

"You know Texas weather. It likes to surprise you. But don't worry, our luck is going to hold with this. Damn it. If we have to, we'll sleep in the damn car, but I don't feel safe driving on these roads."

Especially not with Maddie in the car.

A cold sweat slicked over me, and I realized exactly why I was freaking out, and I had a feeling Maddie figured it out at the same time.

"Oh my God. I'm sorry. Elijah..."

"It's okay. Seriously. We'll be fine."

Because Joy had died in a car accident. Too much rain, hydroplaning, and the car had slammed right into her.

I didn't feel safe driving in this, and I wasn't going to

let Maddie do it either. So we would take our time. And we would let the others know.

"I'm going to get out and see if there's a room. Will you text the others?"

"Okay. Be safe, Elijah. We're going to be okay."

She sounded so calm, soothing, and I shook my head, wanting to reassure her, but she was reassuring me.

The wind was roaring too much for an umbrella to make a difference, and I winced as it rattled the SUV.

"Are you sure you don't want to get out with me?"

"The clouds aren't moving in the right direction, so just hurry. If it looks bad, I'm coming out too."

"Okay. Text the others."

She nodded, and for some strange reason, I wanted to lean forward and brush my lips against hers to let her know everything was okay.

But that would make things even worse.

Rain poured down on me, even though I tried to cover my face, but it didn't matter. Within moments, I was soaked to the bone, and hail battered me. Thankfully there was an overhang, but I knew that the slight covering over my SUV wasn't going to save it much. The insurance was going to be a bitch, but I'd deal with it later. I just needed to keep Maddie safe.

I walked into the small chain hotel, shook off the water while inside the small entryway, and made my way dripping toward the front desk.

Carrie Ann Ryan

The lady gave me a small smile and handed over a towel.

"Sorry about the weather."

"It's not your fault. But I would be so grateful if you had a room."

She winced again, and my hopes plummeted. I didn't relish having to sleep in our car for the night, but there was no way I was driving in this. Not with my phone buzzing in my pocket from all the weather alerts.

"I've only got one left, and it's the honeymoon-esque suite, so I hope that's going to work for you. I wouldn't want anyone else driving in this, but it's all we have."

Ice slid up my spine, and I cringed. "The honeymoon suite?"

She blushed and shrugged. "Well, that's what we call it here. It's our king one-bedroom suite. There is a couch, but there's no pullout. It's a very comfortable couch though, it's made for people with a little extra time, and needing more space. But it only fits two people."

The couch was going to suck for my back, but I would deal with it.

"It comes with complimentary champagne, though."

"That's fine. I don't want to drive out in this."

"I understand. The two staff and I will be staying in overnight."

"I'm sorry about that." And I was, because tonight didn't sound like a good night for anyone.

"It's not your fault. We get overtime for it, and we're

used to it. Don't worry. You'll be taken care of, and so will we. While the restaurant won't be open because we don't have the staff, the diner behind us is, and there is a covered walkway. You can order to go, and they'll bring it right to you. It's the least we could do for you. Don't worry. We'll be safe. You will be dry. And really that's all that matters."

I nodded, and signed the credit card slip, wincing at the total.

The last-minute fees, and the fact that it was the largest and seemingly best room, didn't add up for great spending on budgets, but I would deal. As long as we were dry and not in the middle of the storm, it would be worth it.

"Thank you. Seriously."

"No worries, thank you. Do you need help with your bags or where to park?"

I shook my head. "I've got it on the map," I said as she handed over the sheet, and I stuck it in my pocket, hoping it wouldn't get too wet. And then I made my way back out to the car in the pouring rain, trying to figure out exactly how I was going to tell Maddie that we would be sleeping in one room that only had one bed and not make it sound like I wanted her.

Because the problem was, I did.

And that was always a damn problem.

We stood, drenched, and looked at the so-called honeymoon suite.

"Well..." Maddie began.

"Yeah."

There wasn't much else to say. It was a suite. It had a couch and a small table, as well as a little dining area. There was even a bar area, complete with cheese plate and champagne. I hadn't expected the cheese plate. My stomach rumbled at that, and Maddie let out a soft laugh next to me.

I held back a sigh, and did my best not to look at the bedroom. There were French doors leading towards the area, and the large canopy bed looked ready for whatever came on a honeymoon night.

Because, damn it, there were even rose petals on the fucking floor.

"Do you think they already had the rose petals there, or did they put them down whenever they saw you coming?" Maddie paused. "I didn't mean coming as in... well, you know what I mean. Oh my God."

I looked at her, at our wet suitcases, at the fact that both of us looked like we were drowned rats, and just threw my head back and laughed.

"This is fucking ridiculous."

"Oh yes. Just a little ridiculous. We look like we just jumped into a pool, had mud thrown on us, and decided to mess up this fancy place."

"I didn't realize they even made rooms like this here."

"There must be like a secret code or something. Or maybe she found you mightily attractive. All bearded and broody."

I slid my hand over my five o'clock shadow.

"My brothers are bearded. And broody. I'm none of those."

She looked at me and laughed. "Okay so you have a slight shadow of a beard right now, and you do shave it off often. But you're broody, Elijah. You're always fucking broody."

I blinked. "What?"

"Oh, come on. You hide it well behind your suave sophistication and the fact that you love suits, but all of you Wilder brothers are broody. It's why every person that walks onto our property practically swoons over you. I'm pretty sure it helped you in the business in the first place. Everybody had to get a look at the Wilder brothers, and then they stayed because they liked it."

I shook my head and set down my things. "You've lost your damn mind."

"Maybe."

"Is that what you think works for the Dustin cousins?" I asked, then cursed again.

"What is with you? I am not attracted to Clint."

"Forget I said anything."

"No. If you have a problem, let me know."

"There's nothing going on. I don't have a problem."

"You say that and yet you keep bringing him up. I'm

not going to date, or sleep with, or do *anything* with Clint Dustin. And even if I wanted to, it wouldn't be your fucking business. It wouldn't have anything to do with you. So get over yourself, Elijah Wilder."

My eyes widened at the vehemence in her tone. "Get over myself? You guys were practically drooling over each other while we were at a business event. What do you expect?"

"No, you don't get to do this. You say you're not my boss, so you don't get to act like you care what I was doing. And we weren't drooling over each other. I was happy for the beer. He might have been hitting on me, but it's not like I could tell. I suck at those things, and fuck you. Just fuck you. Why are you even bringing this up?"

"I don't know. It just bothered me seeing him hitting on you."

"Why would it bother you, Elijah? Why? What does men hitting on me have anything to do with you?"

"Because I don't like it. I don't like it when men hit on you, I don't like when they come on to you when you're on the wine tours. I've never fucking liked it."

I hadn't meant to say that. Hell, I hadn't even meant to think that.

"What on earth are you talking about?" she asked, her voice low. "Because it shouldn't matter if you like it or not."

"You're right, it shouldn't. Because we're just brothers to you, right? So it shouldn't matter what I think. What I feel. Because it's stupid. Because I shouldn't be feeling it at all."

I hadn't even had any of that champagne yet, but the words were just flowing out of me. I needed to fucking rein it in.

What was wrong with me?

"What? I can't even keep up with you right now."

"Apparently I can't even keep up with myself."

"You're right, it shouldn't matter who's hitting on me, and I don't know why you're acting like you care."

"Because I've always cared, Maddie. I've always fucking cared who's hit on you. Even when I shouldn't. There. I said it. Surprised?"

She staggered back. "No. You don't get to do that. You don't get to act like you suddenly care about who I've dated and who hits on me. Because you never have."

"I've always cared, but I've been damn good about hiding it. And then I didn't care for a while, because I was in love. Because Joy was everything, but she's not here anymore, and all these feelings are back and hitting me in the face and I can't do anything about it." I was practically yelling at this point, and Maddie looked at me as if I had grown a second head.

"No. Someone told you, didn't they? They told you."

"What?" I asked, confused.

"Who told you? Or maybe you finally fucking saw it, after all this time."

"Saw what? You're the one that said that the Wilders

were your brothers. That you saw us just like having big brothers. So I never did anything. I never said anything. And then there wasn't anything to fucking say. What's your problem?"

She dropped her purse on the floor, the sound echoing in the room. "Are you kidding me right now? When did I say that?"

"When we first moved in. You were talking with Naomi, going over innkeeper shit. You said it loud and clear, and I heard it. I took note. Plus, we were working together, it would have been a bad idea."

She threw her hands up in the air. "Fuck! I said that about everyone but *you*." She put her hands over her mouth, staggering back.

"Are you serious?" I asked, moving forward. I needed to stop, needed to think. Needed to do anything except for what I wanted to do.

"Elijah. Don't."

"Don't what?" I asked softly as I lowered my head, and did the one thing I'd wanted to do for longer than I would admit.

I kissed Maddie, and hoped it wasn't a mistake.

Chapter Seven

Elijah

Maddie slid her hands up my back and I gripped her arms, needing her closer. Thunder shook the room and the lights flickered, but we didn't move away. I kept my mouth on her, doing something I had wanted to do for so long, despite the fact that I had only unconsciously thought about it for all this time. Because this was Maddie. Someone who was all wrong for me and the woman I shouldn't want, yet here I was kissing her—needing her.

And I didn't want to stop.

It didn't matter that I *should* want this to stop.

She groaned into me and I grabbed her hair, pulling

her head back to deepen the kiss. She was so soft, so supple, and I wanted to feel every inch of her.

This would be a mistake in the morning, but right now there were no mistakes, no errors. It was just exactly what we needed.

I tugged on the bottom of her top, and she groaned against me before lifting her arms. The sweater flew over her head, and I went right back to kissing her, to tasting her.

When my hands slid up to cup her breasts over her bra, she moaned, leaning forward to bite my lip.

"Elijah. Should we?" Her voice broke as she spoke, and I growled low.

"Let me. Just say yes."

She stared at me, her eyes wide, full of the same indecision that I knew I held.

Please say yes.

Please say no.

Just please say yes.

She nodded slightly, and I tilted her head up, pinching her chin so she looked directly at me. "I need the words, Maddie. I need to hear it. Yes or no?"

"Yes," she whispered. Barely above a breath. I crushed my mouth to hers, needing more.

She tugged on my shirt and I tore it off, the buttons scattering.

When she laughed, I grinned. "That's a first."

"Well. Eager is good." She cleared her throat, looking down at the tent my cock made in my pants. "Very good."

I gripped myself, squeezing, and her eyes widened. "Oh, it's just the beginning."

I cupped the back of her neck, crushed my lips to hers again, and backed her towards the bed. The back of her legs hit the bed and she sat back, letting out an oof.

From this angle, her face was right at crotch level, and I waited. "Well?"

She rolled her eyes as her hands went to my belt buckle. I stayed her hands, looking down at her.

"Tonight's for you. You don't have to," I began, but she licked her lips.

I slipped my hand down, cupping her breast with my palm before playing with her nipple. My finger slowly played around the edge of the lace and cupped her bra, before tugging it down, releasing her. I pinched at her nipple, the color going from a pale pink to a darker color as blood rushed to the tip. She groaned, and I continued to play with her as she made little mewing sounds, slowly pulling me out of my pants.

"Elijah," she uttered.

I looked down at her, her hair mussed, her lips swollen from my kisses, and swallowed hard. "You're so God damn beautiful."

She shook her head. "I can barely keep up."

"Stop if you must. You don't have to do this."

She shook her head. "But what if I want to?" She gripped my cock and swallowed the tip whole. I closed my eyes and counted as I tried to breathe. She gripped the base of my cock, cupping my balls with her other hand, as she sucked me down, flicking her tongue over the tip as she moved back up. She hollowed her cheeks and hummed on my length, all while bobbing her head. I slid my free hand in her hair, guiding her to go slightly deeper. And when she took me past the back of her throat and swallowed, I closed my eyes and counted so I wouldn't come right then and there.

"Jesus Christ," I mumbled.

She hummed along my dick, licking and sucking. I played with her nipples, kneading her breasts, and when my balls tightened and I was ready to blow, I pulled out and squeezed my cock so I wouldn't come.

"Okay, enough of that."

I moved so my mouth was on her and I was pushing her down on the bed.

With quick movements, I had her bra off, her breasts bouncing on her chest. I continued to suck and lick them, watching the way that her nipples pebbled hard enough that I knew that she would be in pain if she didn't come soon. She pressed her thighs together, trying to create friction, so I pulled down her leggings, throwing them and her panties over my shoulder.

"Elijah!" she called out, as I gripped her hips and pulled her to the edge of the bed. I leaned down, pressing her thighs to the bed, spreading her for me, and lowered my head. I licked her pussy, stroking her clit with the tip of my tongue, knowing that the slight stubble on my face would leave a mark. But I wanted to see my mark on her, my claim. Even if it was just for this one night. I spread her folds, her pink pussy glistening with her own arousal, and I continued to suck. She bucked against me, trying to get away, the orgasm coming soon, but I tightened my hold on her, pinning her to the bed. I blew on her hot heat, and steadily ate her out. She tasted of honey and sweetness and glory, with that slight tart taste that told me that she was going to come soon. And when she did, calling out my name, I didn't stop licking at her, needing her. I slid one finger deep inside her, then another. Her pussy clenched around my fingers, and I kept sucking and licking. And when I entered a third finger inside her, her pussy impossibly tight, I kept going, sitting up so I was laying over her on my forearm, my fingers moving in and out of her.

"I want you to come for me. Fuck my hand. Be a good little girl and come."

Her eyes widened, and she continued to buck on my hand, my thumb sliding gently over her clit before I moved faster. The sounds of wet panting filled the room as I fucked her with my fingers, hard and fast, until both of us were breathing heavily, and she was coming again, her orgasm so intense that she drenched my hand and the sheets.

And then we were shaking, my cock ready to burst, and she pulled at me.

"Elijah...I need...I need. I can't even think. How do you take all of my thoughts away with just one touch?"

She couldn't say anything else, and I just grinned.

That's my girl. That was my fucking girl.

And then I cursed, realization settling in. "I don't have a condom."

"I'm clean. I have an IUD. I promise. I haven't." She let out a breath. "I haven't been with anyone in a few weeks, and I was just tested."

I put that information away for later, knowing that we would have to talk, or maybe we didn't. Maybe I didn't want to.

"I'm clean too."

There had been a few women after Joy. But no one that had been serious, no more than one night, a hard fuck that hadn't gone anywhere. And I was damn clean. When Maddie pulled me towards her and I slid between her thighs, I knew I'd be going bare for the first time in my life.

I swallowed hard. "I've never been without a condom before."

"Me either. But I trust you."

She could trust me with anything, with this, and I was afraid that we were making a mistake. But that was what we were good at, apparently, making mistakes. I kissed her again, knowing she could taste herself on my tongue.

She let out a shocked gasp against my lips as I entered her, going quickly, so I was balls deep, her body pulsating around me.

"Elijah, you're so freaking big." I laughed against her, and she tried to push me away.

"Am I hurting you?" I asked, my hubris sobering quickly.

"No. I just need you to move. I'm at that part where I need to come again, and I didn't think I could come more than once."

"You're already at two. I can make it more."

"That sounds like a dare," she teased.

On edge, I kissed my way up her jaw, nibbling on her earlobe before I pulled back, basking in her, and began to move.

We were hard and fast, learning each other's rhythm, as she slid hot and tight around me. I rolled to my back, so she rode me, her breasts bouncing as she rotated her hips. I plucked at her nipples again, a little harder this time, and I knew she liked it when her breath caught. I gripped her hips harder and pulled out of her, positioning her so she was on all fours in front of me. I slammed into her again, her body clenching as I reared back and slapped her ass. Just one quick slap, to say thank you, and when she moaned, her pussy pulsing around my dick, I knew this was what she wanted, what we both wanted. I slapped her again and again and again until her pretty little ass was all red from my hand. I grinned before leaning over her, biting down on her shoulder gently, and kissing the mark.

"Mine," I growled into her ear, and then I sat back up, gripped her hips, and moved.

Carrie Ann Ryan

We moved together, breaking, sliding against one another, and I could catch my breath, she was coming around my cock and I couldn't hold back any longer. My body shook, emptying into her, coming so hard that I was seeing stars behind my eyelids. And soon we were lying next to each other, my cock still deep inside her, and I was trying to hold back from saying something idiotic.

"Oh," she whispered.

I kissed her again, this time a little more difficult since her back was to my front, and held her, knowing as soon as we spoke for real, the moment would be broken, and there wouldn't be anything else to say.

I had just fucked one of my best friends, and I didn't regret it.

Even though I should.

The next morning we woke up sore, having pleasured each other twice more during the night. The storm had died down, and we needed to head home, but we still hadn't talked. Instead, we showered, this time without touching one another, taking our turns, each of us not meeting the other's gaze.

I had fucked up. Fucked up royally. Because I needed to talk to her, to tell her that I was sorry, or that I wasn't sorry. You shouldn't tell a woman you had just slept with that you were sorry. That was one of the worst things you could do. But what the hell else was I supposed to say?

She stood in the bathroom, putting her hair up in a wet bun, while I finished packing up my meager belongings and toiletries, wondering how the hell we were going to get through the rest of our car ride.

I wasn't *in* love with Joy anymore. I loved who I was with her, who we had been. But I wasn't in love anymore.

I didn't know what kind of man that made me. But I had gone to grief counseling because my brothers and sisters-in-law had forced me into it. My sister had even been the one to sit with me the first time, as she had been through it before. Her first husband died, and she learned to grieve, so she sat by me as I had tried to learn to do the same.

And I tried to find a way through the unending grief that promised me nothing but pain and loss and memories that never went away.

There were people in the group who had been coming for a decade, trying to find answers about the unknown.

Then there were people who were only a year in, a month.

Everybody grieved differently, and they found their ways to be happy again, or to wallow in that unhappiness.

For the first year I had decided I would be the latter. That I wouldn't move beyond who I had been, because it was disrespectful to Joy to want anything else. To want anything more.

But in the end I realized I had been disrespectful to Joy to not want what her name even fucking represented.

I had been going to marry that woman. But she was taken from me. By fate, by rain, by a person driving too fast. In the end she wasn't here. I did not have a future with her. In the second year of my grieving, I allowed myself to touch other women, to see myself in a sexual relationship with them where everyone involved knew what was on the table. They'd walked away satisfied and with what they wanted. They hadn't wanted forever, and I hadn't either.

I hadn't let myself see anything else beyond that. It would be too much.

I had wanted Maddie from the first time I had seen her. Long before Joy, long before I had even gotten to know the Maddie who made me smile.

Long before I had known what Maddie tasted like, what she felt like as she came. And I still wanted her. Even after a night of ecstasy and feeling and everything that could be completely screwed up, I still wanted her. And that realization shocked me. I needed to figure out what to do with that. And what I was supposed to do with myself.

Maddie came out of the bathroom at that moment, her eyes wide, guarded.

"Good morning."

That was a good way to begin, wasn't it?

"Hi."

"Is it wrong that I want to kiss you, but I'm afraid to?"

I hadn't meant to say that, but, honestly, it was the best thing to say in that moment. I wasn't good at this. I never had been, and with Maddie? It was a whole other issue.

"What are we doing?" she asked, and I froze.

"I guess we should talk about that. Because we didn't talk last night."

"I'm leaving, Elijah."

It was as if the world had rocked from beneath me and nothing made sense. I knew it had always been an option. She had been offered a job with Ivy Wines. It was a fantastic offer, one that would lead to great things for her. And she deserved it. She deserved everything she wanted and more because she was brilliant, caring, and always put others first.

And I hated that they had even dared to try to poach her from us. But that was the selfish part of me. That was the part that wanted to touch her again. And perhaps part of the businessman who intellectually didn't want her to go to a competitor. Who wanted her to stay with Wilder Wines and help us flourish. But it was the personal parts, the messy parts, that were screaming inside.

"Don't go."

Okay, not the smartest thing to say, not the thing I should have said at all. But it was out there. And maybe I shouldn't hide anymore.

Her eyes filled with something I couldn't read, but her mouth curled into a sly smile. "Are you going to use your dick to keep me here?" she asked and I burst out laughing, grateful that I could even think about laughing in this situation.

"You know...if I have to." I looked at her and cursed under my breath. "Maddie. Just, don't go. The Wilders need you."

I need you.

I didn't say that out loud.

"We've already mixed work and whatever this is. And it was completely inappropriate. Don't you see? We *work* together. And we just slept together."

"Should I mention that most of the women my brothers are married to work with the Wilders?"

"That doesn't make this right."

"It doesn't make it wrong."

"I don't know what to do, Elijah. I need to think. Because somehow this feels like it came out of left field." She sighed, and I wanted to reach out and touch her, but I knew she wouldn't want me to.

That much I knew about her. It was odd how I could read her in some ways, but in other ways she was hidden from me. And I wanted to peel those layers, to figure out what it all meant.

But that would take time. That would take her not leaving. "Let me think."

"About staying. We want to make you partner. And that has nothing to do with us. I'm not your boss. We work together, so if we fuck up, then it's on me."

She scoffed. "You're a fucking Wilder. And I would be

the one fucking a Wilder." Her lips twitched, and I shook my head.

"Bad joke, Maddie."

"It's all I can do right now. I don't know what I'm supposed to do. I like you, Elijah. And I kind of already blurted that I always have."

Her eyes widened, and I swallowed. "And I told myself that I wasn't supposed to want you. But here we are. I want you, Maddie. I don't know what that means, and it's not fair to either one of us that I don't. But you leaving just feels wrong. It feels like it could be the worst thing that we could do. And I know you still need time to think, and I hate the fact that I'm even putting this on your shoulders. But I want you to stay. For the Wilders, for the wine." I let out a breath. "And I want to figure out what this is. But, if you go to Ivy Wines, it's not that far of a commute. I could, I don't know, see what this means."

She stared at me. "So if I leave, if I leave Wilder Wines so it doesn't complicate the work situation, we'll what, find a way to make this work, whatever this is, long-distance?"

"If we have to. I don't know, Maddie. But doesn't this feel too important just to walk away?"

"I was leaving because I needed something. I needed a reason to stay. And I needed to get away from you," she blurted.

I blinked. "You were going to leave because of me?"

"Maybe? I don't know. Now I'm confusing myself. I just—I need time to think. To think about work, to think about my career, to think about you. Because I was always going to be thinking about you, Elijah. And that's the problem."

"Maybe it's not a problem. Not if we are both aware that we're thinking of each other."

I was grasping at straws here, but I knew if she left, if she decided to go away and never see the Wilders again, that was it for us.

And the selfish part of me didn't want it to be it.

But if we both wanted each other, what was wrong with that?

"I don't know. I just need to think. And now we have a very long and awkward car ride home, where I'm going to put my headphones in, do some work, and pretend. Will you let me pretend for the next two hours?"

I took a step forward and cupped her face. When she didn't move back I counted that as progress.

I lowered my lips to hers, and she shuddered out a breath before kissing me back.

"We'll push pause right now. And then we'll talk. We'll figure it out. Work, the business, us. Everything. Us standing in this random hotel where we need to check out and drive home isn't going to help us at all. So let's push pause."

She nodded tightly.

"Pause works."

I kissed her again, because I couldn't help it. I was that much of a bastard. "Just a pause kiss."

She rolled her eyes. "That's not a thing."

"It is now, Maddie. It is now."

I moved away before I touched her again, and I hoped to hell that this was just a pause.

And not an ending.

Chapter Eight

Maddie

My entire body felt like it was on fire; electrocution probably had the same effect. But that was Elijah. Sending me over the edge even when I didn't realize it.

I had slept with Elijah Wilder. My dreams of it were not as good as it actually had been. It surpassed everything. I couldn't quite believe that this was my life.

It shocked me. Honest to God, I was all up in my head and I couldn't focus. But I needed to. I needed to work, plan, and meet with wine clubs and the multiple tour groups coming in through the day.

While there were other people who worked on the

tours with me, today was a long day because I had missed so much time while working with the festival.

This was part of my job that I actually loved. Nothing was ever the same. Yes, there were always similar questions, and people that could fit into certain categories, but I was surprised more often than not. And I liked meeting with people. I just liked people. Which was at odds with most of the Wilder brothers. Though Elliot, the youngest brother, liked to pretend that he was bubbly and great with people, I knew sometimes he just wanted to hide away. Elijah was even good at the whole schmoozing thing, very good if I was honest with myself, but I wasn't going to think about that. Would I still be doing this job if I became partner? Would I be able to work with people? Would I want to?

These were the questions and worries I had. No, that was a lie. Because I would find my place, where I fit in, if I were partner. No, all of this worry centered around one person, and that was why I was so conflicted. Because on one hand I needed to leave. On the other, something big had happened—something much more could still happen.

And I couldn't focus on it. No, I needed to worry about what I could control. And that was work.

"Hey, Maddie? Are you ready for your 10:00 a.m.?"

I grinned over at Jay, our vintner, nodding. "Yep. I love 10:00 a.m. wine tastings. Because you start the day off right."

"Yes, they're usually the ones that want to do multiple things during the day, or just really like their wine."

"Yep. And then we'll leave them to Kendall and her kitchen so they get fed nice, right before they go off to the next winery. But ours will always be the best."

Ours. Because I worked here. And they wanted to make me partner. How had that happened?

It didn't seem real. It would solve many problems though, problems I had made myself because of my choices with Elijah.

"Are you okay?"

I blinked out of my own thoughts and looked over at Jay. "Of course, I am."

"If you're sure. You just had a weird look on your face."

I just shrugged it off, knowing I needed to get my head in the game. "Just a long travel day yesterday. But I'm doing great."

Was my voice getting more high-pitched? I felt like I was getting more high-pitched.

Jay gave me a weird look, then shrugged. "Well, I heard that everything at the festival was good. Elijah seems happy, if not as jumpy as you are." He narrowed his gaze at me.

I held up my hands. "Anyway, I have to go get to that tour. I'll save you some wine."

He snorted. "What happened at this festival?"

I wasn't about to answer that. "I drank a lot of beer. That's it. I feel like I cheated on my wine."

This time he laughed, shaking his head. "You're right. How dare you have fun at a brewery. We're winos."

"I would say I'm a booze-o, but that sounds weird. How about I just like fancy food, bar food, beer, wine, liquor, brandy—anything."

"Brandy is liquor."

"Yes, but I was on a roll."

"If you say so," he repeated, studying my face.

I picked up my folder and scurried out of the office, towards where the tour would meet up.

We were booked all month with daily tours, and I was thrilled. A couple of people that were coming later that day were repeats. Meaning they liked our tour enough, and they wanted to come back. Because, the thing was, you could have our wine by just coming into our restaurant. Into our bar. You didn't need to do the tour. If you knew what you wanted and you knew the history behind the Wilder brothers and our wines, you wouldn't need to join us. But people wanted to. They enjoyed the experience. And I felt like I was part of that.

That's why I felt a kinship to this place, and why becoming partner would be such a huge thing. Because my responsibilities would change, but I could make my role my own. Each of the brothers, as well as Alexis and Kendall, had made their place here. They didn't have a set guidelines.

I had already gone over the full offer, and everything else they gave me to look at before I made my decision. It was everything that I could ever want. It was even more than what Ivy Wines could have promised.

And that was excluding the emotional connections I already had.

This was perfect for me.

It was a lot of money. It would change everything.

And it meant I would probably stay.

Perhaps not for Elijah, because I wouldn't let myself promise that. But with him.

And that was either an obstacle, or a bonus. The fact that I couldn't tell right away told me I still needed time to think. Or at least talk it out.

That meant I had to do the one thing I had been avoiding since I'd gotten back.

Talk with the girls. But first, I had to do my job. The reason that I was even up for partner to begin with.

I turned the corner and waved at the group of people waiting. "Hello there. I'm Maddie, and I will be your tour guide for the day."

"Hi, Maddie," a couple of people said at once, and I grinned.

"Okay. Let's talk wine, and those Wilders." I winked as I said it, and a couple of people laughed, and then I made sure they were all checked in, and started my day.

Because this was what I was good at. And I needed to remember that.

———

By the time I was finished with my fourth tour of the day, my feet hurt, I was hungry, and I was ready for something other than our normal repertoire of wines. I didn't drink every tour. Sometimes I sipped, or even spit into a bucket. It wasn't pretty, but you needed to. Especially if you were going to have that much wine all day.

It was just how wine tours worked.

I didn't want to get drunk while working. I didn't like to be drunk at all. I liked having full access to my faculties while tasting my favorite wines.

I made my way to the employee tasting area, wondering what food Kendall had sent up for us today. It was our girls' evening, something I needed, and that meant we had this area for our private times. Other staffers could come in and out if they wanted, but it was after hours, and they all knew that this was a place that we liked to hang out. We could have met at any of each other's houses, or in other parts of the building, but our meetups had started here, and I liked it.

It would be something I would miss if I left.

And that was something else to add to my what-if columns.

Kendall and Alexis were already there, laughing at something over their phones.

"Well, hello there," I said with a smile.

Kendall waved. "You're here. I made appetizers for the

evening, rather than a full dinner. I know last time we had a bunch of different kinds of soups and breads, but I always enjoy small plates and tapas."

I rubbed my hands together. "I'm starving."

"That's because you didn't come in for lunch. You just went from tour to tour," she chided, as Alexis narrowed her eyes at me. "You know the rules. You need to take care of yourself."

"I wasn't hungry."

And I was stressed. Not that I was going to get into that.

Alexis sighed. "Are you going to tell us why you're stressed? Because you're far more fidgety than usual."

I paused as I reached for a cream cheese and bacon pinwheel with some sort of seasoning and relish that I wasn't sure would go well together, but I trusted Kendall completely. "I'm fidgety?"

"In a good way," Alexis added.

"Okay, that's weird." I popped the morsel into my mouth and groaned in pleasure.

Alexis cleared her throat. "Well, I think she likes it."

Kendall laughed and made notes on her tablet. "That's good. I'm going to add that sound to our checkboxes. Do you orgasm while eating this? I think that's a yes for Maddie."

I flipped her off and took another one. "Oh, shut up. This is amazing. Are you adding it to the menu?"

"I was thinking about adding it to your tour list. Or the bar. At least for catering."

"Yes, to all of that," I said, as Alexis clapped her hands. "Oh my gosh. This at weddings? I'm going to gain like forty pounds and I'm excited about it."

"It is the best," I added.

"I'm glad. It's the chutney."

"Don't tell me what's in it. Because then I would pretend I could make it myself, and we know I can't."

"That is true," Kendall teased. "You try, but sometimes, you end up with fires in the kitchen."

I narrowed my eyes. "That was one time."

"Yes. One time, and we'll never let it go."

I flipped her off as there was laughter behind us, and I turned to see Bethany and Lark walking into the room with Trace, Bethany's bodyguard, behind her.

Bethany started dating Everett over two years ago. And she was practically a Wilder already. They were taking their time with their relationship, because it wasn't as if they could just do whatever they wanted without being in the public eye. Bethany was an Oscar winner, and sometimes it surprised me that she was part of our group. She was so down to earth, and yet one of the most sought-after actresses of our time. Her best friend, Lark, a Grammy award winning, singer-songwriter, wrote songs that meant the world to me, so the fact that they were both in this room still left me starstruck sometimes. But I always pushed that aside because they were my friends first.

I glanced behind them at the scowling Trace and waved. He didn't wave back, but he did do a quick search of the room, and I just shook my head. I hated the fact that even though we were in here, and we should be safe, Trace had to worry.

But he was doing his job, and even though she was here with friends, Bethany's safety took priority.

"Are you going to join us, Trace?" Kendall asked.

Bethany rolled her eyes. "You've already checked out this place. We're good. Come and sit and have a drink with us. You're off the clock and you know it."

Trace just sighed and pulled out his phone. "No, I have to meet with Elliot about something. And then I'm going to head to the house. I promise, I'll enjoy myself tonight. Maybe even have a beer. Watch out."

"A beer?" I asked, letting out a shocked and clearly fake gasp.

Trace just rolled his eyes. "Sue me. I like beer."

"I can't believe you would say that in a place of wine," Lark said, her voice a little breathy, a small smile on her face brightening her eyes. "I mean, it's sacrilege."

"I can't right now with you guys. It's exhausting."

"What's exhausting?" East asked, as the handyman of the Wilders walked inside and glared. "Are they annoying you? Then kick them out."

"You could try, but we could take you, East," Kendall said as she narrowed her eyes.

"Whatever, I need to fix something back in the kitchen. Is it going to bother you that I'm here?"

I pressed my lips together and watched the way that he was purposely not looking at Lark. Maybe I was just seeing things, but for some reason it looked as if the two of them were not looking at each other on purpose.

Or maybe I just wanted to see something that wasn't there. Because I knew that East liked her music. I had heard it playing from his earphones once before. Yet I had never seen them talk.

And, maybe if I thought about that long enough, I wouldn't have to focus on what I needed to talk to the girls about.

"It's after five, do it tomorrow," Alexis said softly. "Take some time for yourself. You're allowed to do that."

East rolled his eyes, and then nearly staggered back as Trace pulled him out of the room. "Come on, it's girl talk. Let them have it. We want nothing to do with that."

"I guess," he grumbled as the two of them left.

I just laughed, shaking my head. "They're exhausting."

"You have no idea," Lark grumbled, and I met Bethany's gaze, who just shrugged over her best friend's head and leaned forward for a glass of wine.

"This looks amazing. Thank you for scheduling this. I love it when I'm here during girls' time."

"You've been on location for so long, it's great to have you back," Kendall said.

"Now, tell me everything that's happened since we've been gone," Bethany ordered, and Alexis met my gaze.

"Why don't you tell us what happened with you and Elijah on the trip?"

Everyone stared at me, and my eyes widened. "Excuse me?" I squeaked. "Nothing. Nothing happened."

"Okay, well, that's a lie," Lark said with a laugh.

I threw my hands up in the air. "I'm just so confused. We slept together. We freaking slept together, and now I'm supposed to act like everything's normal. But it's not normal. Because you guys want to make me partner, and yet if I did that, then would I be sleeping with my partner? Or is that just complicating everything? And I like Ivy Wines, but I love you guys more, and it just feels like no matter what I do I'm going to make the wrong decision. And I hate myself."

I rambled on and told them everything that happened during the trip, the storm, and Elijah wanting more.

They stared at me, eyes wide, mouths agape, not a single person even moving.

"Finally," Lark said. "I mean, we all saw the connection between those two, right? I'm rarely even here and I noticed."

"You're not wrong," Kendall added.

"I know you guys all knew I had a crush on him. But did you know he had feelings for me?"

Alexis shrugged. "Not really. Mostly because he's good at hiding his emotions. There was only one time where I could truly read his face, and even then it was easy to miss."

Joy. We all knew it was Joy. And that was just one more ghost in the conversation that I couldn't deal with.

"Well, are you leaving? Would it be easier for you to go to Ivy Wines?" Kendall asked in her no-nonsense voice. And that's why I loved her. Because she threw it out there, she asked, and now I had to deal.

"I don't know. I didn't say yes to them yet, because they know it's a big decision. And I still have a couple of weeks to make that decision, but I also want to make sure that I manage this festival and make sure we kick ass."

"Of course, we're going to kick ass, and you're a huge part of that." Alexis sipped her wine and then set down her glass. "And you know that. But we don't want to hold you back. But I will say I want you here. You living and working a couple of hours away would not be fun. And that's the lamest way to say that, isn't it?"

"I don't know. And I also don't know if I'm ready to commit that much money to being partner. And it would change everything. But it's a big thing and I love you guys for asking. I just don't know what I'm supposed to do. And add in Elijah, and the fact that it was amazing. A-freaking-mazing. And yet, if it all blows up it will do so spectacularly and ruin everything."

"What do you want?" Lark asked, her voice soft.

I looked at all of them, downed the rest of my wine, and set the glass down. "I have done everything by the book. I have worked my ass off, and now I'm afraid I've put myself into this box. I have done my best to be the best at what I do. I've tried not to hold anyone else back, but I've been staying in the same position, not moving forward, not moving back. I didn't let myself feel anything for Elijah before because it was just going to hurt. You all saw that. And I hated the pity." They all started to speak at once, but I held my hand up. "I know. I know you didn't mean it, but I felt it. I felt it every time he was in the room and you guys tried your best not to look at me. It was ridiculous. I didn't automatically earn his feelings back. That's not how they work. Unreciprocated feelings are that way for a reason. But apparently, they weren't so unreciprocated. And I have to come to terms with that. I was ready to leave because I didn't want to stay anymore. I didn't want to *not* grow."

I didn't want to be near Elijah and not have him.

I didn't say that last part aloud. That was what I'd hidden deep down for the past two years and did my best to never think about. I'd tried to move on, and I had. Only I'd failed so completely I hadn't realized it until his mouth was on mine and I wasn't pulling away.

"What if I stayed?"

I hadn't meant to say that aloud, but my friends answered anyway.

"We want you to. You could grow with us."

I looked at Kendall and swallowed. "I have worked so hard with the Wilders. With this company. And then if I let myself..." I let out a shaky breath, knowing I was saying the craziest thing I'd ever said in my life, but maybe I needed to. "Maybe I should do what I've wanted to for years."

Bethany leaned forward. "And that is?"

"Have Elijah. Even for a moment."

"Now that is what I'm talking about," Lark said with a grin. "You need to. I've seen the way you two are with each other."

"And if I mess it all up? Well, it's mine to mess up. Because I'm so tired of being safe. I just don't want to ruin Wilder Wines in the process."

"You won't. We won't let you. So, does this mean yes just to Elijah? Or yes to being partner?"

I bit my lip. "Yes to Elijah, and let me work on the financials before I say yes to being partner."

They all cheered and threw their arms around me, and I held them close, hoping to hell I knew what I was doing.

Chapter Nine

Elijah

This day was never-ending. All I wanted to do was drop everything and go to the office and see if Maddie was there. But she needed a moment. She needed space. And we were working, so that meant I had to step back and not force myself into her presence. I needed to prove that we could work together, and therefore that was what I was trying to do.

But all I wanted was to see her. Even if it was a bad idea. Thankfully, my brothers were working all day and didn't have time for me. They were focused on the upcoming festival, but I knew we would meet soon. We would go through what we needed to do, and get things done. For now, they didn't need me. I didn't have to hide my feelings, or the fact I was so fucking off-kilter that I couldn't focus on anything.

Instead, I worked, I focused as best I could, I planned, and then I found myself in my car and on my way to Maddie's place before I could think. She could tell me to go. But I needed her to be there. *I just needed her.*

I didn't know how this had happened, how I had ended up in this position, but I wasn't going to think too hard about it. Not right then.

I pulled into her driveway and noticed her neighbor sitting on the porch, knitting. The older woman waved at me, wrapped up in a blanket, and I nodded at her, worried it was getting a little chilly as the sun went down. But she looked comfortable. I'd check in about her with Maddie later. Just to be sure. I knew that Maddie watched over her neighbors. She was a good person, and always cared for them.

I knocked on the door and waited, wondering what the hell I was going to say.

When it flew open, her eyes wide, her hair wild, alarm spread through me.

"What's wrong? Are you okay? Is someone in there?"

I moved to go inside and she put her hand on my chest. With that one motion I froze, looked down at her delicate hand on my chest, and I put my hand over hers, covering it completely.

"What is going on, Maddie?"

"You're here. How are you here?"

The alarm that had shot through me began to dissipate as I stared at her, another feeling sliding into me. "I drove here."

Well, not the most eloquent, but it was the truth.

Her lips twitched. "No one's in the house, just me, and now you." She pulled me inside. When the door closed behind me, I swallowed hard, my gaze intent on hers. I loved her house, the homey feel, the way that there was always a space for guests. I had been here a few times over the years, but never like this, never when I wanted to press her against the wall and taste every inch of her.

There was a problem for me, and I knew it. "I know how you got here—I see your car—but, well, I was just here to gather up a few things and then I was going to come to you. After work."

My heart sped as her words finally began to make sense in my head.

"You were going to come to me." I paused. "For what I think you're talking about?"

Her lips twitched. "Yes. I just...I wanted to see you. To, well..." She let out a breath, moved back and pointed towards a stack of papers. "I think I can make the financials work. This is my home. I love it here. And I'm doing this for me. For my future, for my strengths, and for what I want to do. I have a few more things to go over, but I want to become partner. With the Wilders."

I didn't realize I was grinning so wide until my cheeks

began to hurt. I moved forward and cupped her face. "Really?"

I slid my hands down her sides, gripped her hips, and picked her up. When I spun her around her kitchen, she laughed, wrapping her arms around my neck. When she wrapped her legs around my waist, I groaned.

I pressed her against the edge of the kitchen counter, her forehead on mine. "You're going to stay," I whispered.

"For me. For the Wilders."

Disappointment began to slide through me before she tightened her legs. "And, while I'm here, I want to try to make *this* work. Whatever it is. I'm giving myself that chance. I'm not good about what happens next."

Before she could ramble herself out of saying yes again, I tightened my hold on her and crushed my lips to hers.

She moaned against me as I slid my tongue along hers. "Not in my kitchen. I have a thing about sex in kitchens. It just seems so unsanitary."

I pulled back and laughed. "Okay. I guess you're going to have to show me your bedroom, because your couch in there is way too small for me to taste that pussy of yours. I'm going to need room to spread out."

She blushed completely, her face going a pretty scarlet. It made me wonder what color her nipples were right then. "So. No talking right now? Just this?"

"I have waited all day. All I've wanted to do was find

you in the wine cellar and fuck you over a barrel. What kind of man does that make me?"

"A kinky wino?" she asked. I gripped her hips and picked her up off the counter. She squealed and giggled, and she held onto me tightly. I somehow made it to her bedroom down the hall.

I kept kissing her, nearly tripping and dropping her, but we just laughed, and I let myself be.

We were both in our heads far too much these days, so in this moment I was just going to be.

I gently let her down, her feet touching the floor as I continued to kiss her, to taste her. "You're so beautiful," I whispered, pushing her hair from her face.

"I'm a wreck. But thank you."

"If this is what a wreck is, I like it. Though I think we can do one better."

She raised a brow. "You said you liked it, and now you want to change me?"

"I'm just thinking you're wearing too many clothes."

She rolled her eyes, but still slid her hand down to cup my crotch.

I rolled my eyes. "See, I think you like it."

"If I'm going to get naked, you better get naked too."

We kissed again, gently exploring one another.

We had been hard and fast the first time, and then lost in our own memories the times after that for that one night. But this was slower. A beginning. A choice we were both making, damn the consequences.

We stripped each other slowly, getting to know one another's lines, each other's likes.

She let out a sharp breath when I sucked on her neck and slid my hand between her legs. She arched into me as I slowly delved between her folds with first my fingers, then my tongue. She was gentle, sweet, and came with such beauty that it made me want more.

I wasn't a poet, wasn't a romantic, but I wanted to show her how much I wanted her. How much I craved her.

She was an obsession, a need.

Something I hadn't let myself want or think about in far too long.

But I didn't want to think about what I had missed, what I was coming into again, I only wanted to think about now.

I teased her, watching her come once more, before I slid into her, our fingers tangled with one another's, as I seated myself inside her.

"Whoa," she muttered under her breath, and I grinned, capturing her moan with my mouth.

My hands continued to move, caressing her breasts, her hips. She wrapped her legs around me, moving with the rhythm. We were slower this time, oh so slow. Her pussy clamped around my cock, holding me close. I kept moving, loving the way she flooded around me, her orgasm building and building until she was whispering my name, groaning it, and I followed, unable to hold back, unable to not want more.

Once again we hadn't used a condom, once again we had just gone full force.

I was smarter than this, we both were. But for some reason it was as if we were living in our dream world, where there were no consequences.

Only real life was a consequence, and we were going to have to talk.

But I just held her as we came down, and kept kissing her, wanting more.

All I wanted was more.

"You're so fucking beautiful."

"I'm sweaty and disgusting and covered in you. But sure."

"Now I'm getting all caveman here and liking that you're covered in me."

"Okay, that's gross. Sorry. I am not a girl who likes to be sticky. I need a shower."

I raised a brow, before I jumped off the bed and pulled her with me.

"How do you have so much energy?"

"I just had sex with you, and I'm still on my high, of course I have energy."

She rolled her eyes as she piled her hair on the top of her head, and we jumped in the shower.

I let out a quick gasp as the water turned on, icy before it got hot. "We need to bring East out here to check your pipes." I paused, looked at her, and we both burst out laughing.

"No, no. I do not have a brothers kink. One Wilder is far more than I need."

"I would think I'm just enough."

I reached around and slapped her ass, before I gripped her, spreading her cheeks. She groaned into me, my finger playing with her hole, gently entering in and out of her, using her wetness.

"I think I'm a little too tired for more."

"I'm not a young teenager anymore. It's going to take me a little bit longer to recover. I just wanted to see if you would push me away."

"Because you want anal?" she asked with a laugh.

"Well, we could put it on the table."

"So you want to fuck my ass while I'm on a table?" She lathered up the loofah and washed me first, her brow raised.

It was such a gentle and unconscious act, even as we were talking about something others thought was taboo.

This felt right, normal. As if we'd done it a thousand times.

That should have worried me, but it didn't. "I'll take you on a plane, I'll take you on a train, I'll take you anywhere you want, and then I'll rhyme some more even when it's not the greatest." I frowned. "Wait, I need to work on that."

She rolled her eyes. "Please don't do an anal rhyme

poem. As eloquent as you usually are...that was bad." She snorted and I agreed. She'd made me loopy, and that was so unlike me, I felt like I should be worried. "And, we should probably talk."

"Damn it. I guess you're right. Talking's good. But now that we know that anal could be on the table, in the shower, or on the bed, I'm good."

"No anal in the shower. That is how you fall. And you'd break a hip."

"Yes, I can just see it now. The paramedics come and ask how exactly did you break your hip."

"Yes, we're not going to have that. Sorry."

I rolled my eyes, kissed her softly, and we both rinsed. And then I got dressed again, watching her do the same. While I was sad that I was no longer watching her naked, I was glad that she had covered up. It was hard to think when she was naked.

"So," she said after a moment. "This is what we're doing."

I ran my hands over my face, trying to catch up. While we had been joking and just going through our desires a few moments ago, it was a harsh step back to reality. To remembering that though I smiled and joked, I hadn't been that guy for the past couple of years. It was like putting on an ill-fitting suit, one that I used to wear so often.

It still fit, in some places. But not everywhere. "I haven't really dated since..."

She paled. "I'm sorry."

I cursed under my breath. "No, don't be. We should talk about it. Her. Joy was my friend too. And it's been the elephant in the room that we haven't talked about." I cursed again. "But you and I have been friends forever." The sharp realization of exactly what that meant hit me like a train, and I staggered back. "I talked about Joy with you." When she gave me that small, sad smile, I shook my head. "Fuck. I talked about Joy with you," I repeated. "And you—this whole time. Oh my God, Maddie."

"Yes, it was a special kind of hell, but you and I were friends, and Joy and I were also friends. So, what was I supposed to do? Not talk about you with her and her with you? I wanted you to be happy with her. I wanted that forever for the two of you. But here we are, and I don't know what to do."

"Just tell me that I'm a fucking idiot and that I'm selfish. I'm so sorry."

She leaned forward and cupped my face. "Stop it. You were feeling. You were talking about your feelings with me. Which is insane because you and your brothers do that only with each other. I was honored to actually have that. And yes, it sucked, because I had feelings that I knew weren't reciprocated then. But that's on me. You wanting to have happiness and wanting to talk about it is just you. How am I supposed to be mad about that?"

"I can still feel like an asshole about it."

"And I can still feel like an asshole for being happy in

this moment with you. And knowing Joy isn't. We'll always have that between us. And that's something we're going to have to work through. Along with the mountain of other things that makes this very complicated, Elijah."

She lowered her hands and I pushed her hair back from her face again, wanting to stare into those eyes of hers, and followed my thumbs along her strong cheekbones.

"I want to do this. I don't want to hide it."

"Good, because the girls already know."

I closed my eyes and sighed before I grinned. "Of course they do."

"I didn't know this was supposed to be a secret."

I frowned at her. "I just told you I didn't want it to be a secret. Because, like you said, we have hurdles and mountains and all those other metaphors, about this. We might not know exactly *what* it is, because if we put a label on it, at this stage, we'd be setting each other up for failure. So we're going to figure out exactly what this is together, and I'm not going to hide it from my brothers, you're not going to hide it from the girls. And you're going to stay."

She smiled at me then, and relief slammed into me.

She was going to stay. Thank God.

"Yes. I'm not going anywhere. I'm home."

Warmth spread through me and I slid my fingers over her lips, just wanting to touch her again. "I'm going to take you out. To dinner. On a date. Because I know we are very compatible sexually, and in many other ways, but I want to make sure that I don't take advantage of the fact that we work together. That I see you every day."

I was going to treasure those moments. Every single one of them. Because I knew without a doubt how swiftly they could be taken away.

"We have the festival. We have all that planning. And more paperwork to go through, and whatever plans are required for me to come on as partner. There's a lot to do, Elijah. Taking just these moments is okay, too."

"We can do both." I didn't know why this was so important to me, but I needed her to understand.

"We're going to mess this up," she said solemnly.

I shook my head. "Not if we try."

Of course, I had lost before when I had tried, but I wasn't going to say that out loud, and thankfully she couldn't read those thoughts from studying my face.

She opened her mouth to say something, before she suddenly tore away from me, slammed opened the back door, and ran.

I followed her as she ran towards a woman with gray hair, nearly white in the moonlight, and I cursed as I stepped on a briar, but kept moving.

"Martha? What are you doing outside?"

The woman looked over, and I saw the blankness in her gaze as she shook her head. "I'm sorry. I'm just, I wanted a walk."

Maddie pressed her lips together and moved forward. "It's dark outside. You should stay home."

"No, no. I need a walk."

"Mom!" A young man called as he ran. "I'm sorry, Maddie. She got away from me."

"Maddie?" I asked, and she shook her head, but I knew she would explain later.

We helped the other man get his mother back into her house, as Maddie whispered fiercely under her breath.

I saw the sadness etched on her face.

When we made it back to her backyard, the creek burbling behind us, Maddie slid her arms around my waist. I hugged her tightly to me.

"She's getting worse. I'm glad her son is here now, but I hate her being alone."

"That was scary. I'm glad you saw her."

"Me too. But you see? I can't go. I can't move. People need me."

I need you.

I didn't say that. But when I kissed her softly, the moonlight shining, I had to wonder—who did Maddie need?

Chapter Ten

Maddie

From: Elijah
To: Maddie
Subject: Tonight?
I promised dinner. But we might need to postpone. We could still have dessert though. A sweet, delicate dessert. Or perhaps something a little hotter? You decide.

I blinked, trying to decipher exactly what he was saying. Did he want me to be the dessert? Or was he in the mood for cake?

I just shook my head and then clicked the next email.

From: Elijah
To: Maddie
Subject: Re: Tonight?
Just thinking about you. I'll stop with the weird emails. I know I could text, but this is our thing.
Or maybe I'm losing my mind.
See you soon.

I ducked my head, blushing.

Well. It seemed that Elijah truly enjoyed flirting in emails.

And I was not a writer. I could say what I needed to in my tours, and I could think of pretty funny little quips that made sense to the people I was with. But I was not good at putting down my feelings in an email. And Elijah was. Apparently.

And to think, this odd warm sensation, these emails all began with someone replying all about the festival that we were planning.

We needed to work today as a group—at least, Elijah, Evan, and I. Elliot would be joining in as well, since he helped with event planning. This would be a huge endeavor, and I was excited about it.

And yet all I could think about was the fact that I was staying.

That soon I would sign paperwork, and have a huge stake in the Wilders.

And tangled all in that was Elijah.

But I was kidding myself. Elijah had always been tangled within that. There was no changing that.

And part of me didn't want to change it at all.

"Maddie?"

I turned to see Lark standing outside my office, a notebook in her hand, her hair in a braid off the side of her shoulder, with a cute little wide-brimmed hat on her head.

"Hi there, Lark. You look adorable today."

She looked down at her dress, her cowgirl boots, and shrugged.

"I wasn't trying to. I sort of just slapped something together. I'm looking quite singer-songwriter in the wheat fields today."

I snorted. "Maybe, but it works for you."

"Perhaps. Or perhaps I'm trying too hard." She winced and shook her head. "Ignore me. I saw an article online and I hate accidentally reading things about me that aren't actually for me. I know you're busy today, and have a tour group later, but do you think I could join? Would that be against the rules if I just sat back and watched? I don't need to drink any wine or anything, I just want to experience it."

"Are you going to write a song about wine tours?" I asked, oddly curious.

She shook her head. "I don't think so. It's more that I want to people-watch. Which sounds kind of rude. But sometimes I just need to do something that I'm not used to. And, I don't know. I think maybe I'm bored." She snorted. "Which isn't nice considering I'm here to visit my friend. But Bethany and Everett are finally getting a moment together since he couldn't come out last week like he was planning."

I grimaced. "Because Elijah and I were on the festival circuit."

"I don't think anyone begrudges you for that. Especially with how it turned out."

I knew she was teasing me as she said it, but I winced. "I still feel bad though."

"Bethany's here for a month. And then they go off together. It's okay. They didn't get to see each other for six days. That's it. I promise you they're fine."

"I still feel guilty though."

Between Bethany being on location or having to be in LA for certain things with work, Everett was away from the Wilder property more often than not. But when he had to be here for certain things, like when one of his brothers needed to be offsite, Everett couldn't be gone for too long. It wasn't often, and in reality it wasn't as if the two of them spent much time away from each other, but I still felt bad.

"Stop with the guilt. If they had a problem, they would talk about it, and find a solution. I just like to give them some alone time together. Because they deserve it."

"If you're sure."

Lark smiled. "I am. Plus, this gives me the option of not being the third wheel."

"You know you don't have to stay at their place. You're always welcome to stay at mine. Or in one of the free cabins."

There were multiple cabins on the property that weren't being used at the moment. There wasn't always space, but they kept an empty cabin or two for emergencies. Or just because East was working on them.

There were also a few rooms at the inn itself that Lark could stay in.

"That's sweet. But I'm okay. Plus, I'm not about to stay with you, if Elijah's going to be over. That's just me being a fifth wheel at that point."

I blushed. "Oh. Well, I guess that's true."

"You're damn right it is. But it is quite cute. Seriously, you are adorable."

"I don't know about that. Awkward maybe."

"You feel awkward? Are you still in that awkward stage where you're figuring out what love is and what your relationship could be, but you don't want to make too much of it?"

"Are you going to write a song about this?" I asked with a laugh.

"I might. Those first few days of figuring out who you are versus who you were, added in with who you could be together, are always interesting."

"Especially when you're figuring it out with someone that you've known for years."

Lark's eyes sparkled. "You know, I might just have to write something." She winked, and I shook my head.

"I don't know. Because every time I heard it, I'd think of Elijah, and that could get interesting."

"Only the best kinds of interesting. Seriously though, I'm already thinking about maybe buying a house out here. Would that be weird?"

I blinked at the pivot in the conversation before I grinned. "You would move out here? To outside San Antonio?"

"I should be able to write anywhere." She paused. "Sometimes I can't write anywhere, but that's a whole other discussion." She quickly moved on before I could ask her exactly what that meant. "But Bethany's out here more often than not, and when I'm not touring, I'm only living in LA because of her. Which sounds pathetic, but she's my best friend and I like to be near her. I can put a studio in whatever house I am in. Which is such a privilege, and it sounds like a first-world problem because it is, but it's work. It's my office. I don't know. People write everywhere. Shania Twain even recorded a song with Lionel Richie on a tropical resort or something like that."

"I saw that in her documentary. It was pretty cool."

"Right? We can do anything. But, I don't know, maybe a change of scenery would be nice. I just want to be near my friends."

"I hope you know that I count you as one of my friends. Which is kind of cool in a fangirl sense."

Lark rolled her eyes. "We are friends. And that means soon we need to have some of that wine, and you can dish about Elijah. I'm going to live vicariously through all of your relationships."

"I take it you and Harry aren't dating," I teased, mentioning the latest person that the tabloids had set her up with.

This time Lark burst out laughing. "We walked into a coffee shop next to each other because we wanted coffee. We didn't even come from the same direction. I don't even really know him other than I've spoken to him twice. But he's number one on the charts right now, and I'm number two, so therefore we must want to duet together, or we have a rivalry, or we're sweethearts at the top. Either way, he did knock me down the charts. He should have bought me my coffee."

"I have no idea how you deal with it. People asking about your love life and making up different things about you."

"Well, we all thought that you and Elijah should be together long before you were, so maybe you have a taste of that."

I shook my head. "No, I put my own stresses and

complications on my life. Maybe the world had a little bit to do with it, but it's nothing like yours."

Something shadowed her eyes and I regretted even bringing it up. "You're right, but I deal. And no, I'm not dating Harry. Or Matt, or Ryan. Or the other Ryan. Or Chris. Or any of the Chrises. I am single and happy and not writing music about my love life. Which I know is a shock because that's what the world thinks I write about."

"Well, I think I was more shocked that you would go out and get your own coffee. Don't you have staff for that?"

"It's true. I like to run my own errands sometimes, though. Now, will you let me go on your tour?"

"Of course. But you realize that people might recognize you, right?"

"I'm going to try to stand off to the side. And act casual. We'll see. Most people know my voice, and a little bit of me, but I'm not on social media much. Everybody knows Bethany, but I am less recognizable."

I wasn't sure I believed her on that, but it didn't matter. Because Lark wanted to live life a little, and I was going to do my best to help.

The tour went well, everyone recognized her and she smiled and took pictures, looking adorable in her pixieish way, and then those people went off, bought wine, and had a story to tell about that time they came to the Wilder Retreat and met a celebrity and went on a wine tour with her. Lark seemed down to earth, which I knew she was, but now others would see it as well.

Lark went off to "daydream" as she put it, and I went back to work, going over festival prep. We had two nights with the festival, during which we had to plan dinners and events, and that meant we needed music, dancing, food, and, of course, wine. Everybody had their role to play. I was so in the zone with work, that when Nathaniel came up, he startled me. I didn't know how long he had been standing there.

I looked up at him and gave him a soft smile, feeling awkward as hell.

"Maddie, congrats about the festival. We're playing. I hope you know that. Is that going to be weird?"

I shook my head, feeling oddly relieved that he didn't reach out and try to touch me, or look angry or uncomfortable. I don't know why he would be angry, but here I was, trying something with Elijah, just days after Nathaniel and I had broken up. It didn't matter that we hadn't slept together for weeks before. The timing was still weird.

"I'm happy. You guys always bring a crowd and make people dance. That's what we want. We want people to leave here and remember the Wilders."

"Don't you worry. We've got that down." He cleared his throat. "I just wanted to let you know though, that Jeanette? Well, we're sort of seeing each other."

Jeanette was his bassist, and I knew they had been friends for a while. I didn't feel a single ounce of jealousy, and that was probably a very large problem in my relationship with Nathaniel to begin with.

"Really?" I asked.

He stuffed his hands in his pockets, rocked back on his heels. "Yeah. I hope that's okay. I mean, it's just, well, timing and everything."

I shook my head and smiled, this time letting it reach my eyes. "I'm excited for you. You guys have always been good friends. And I don't know, maybe you guys would fit better together than we had." I winced. "That sounded wrong."

"No, you're right. You and I are better as friends. Or workmates, whatever." He cleared his throat. "I, uh, kind of overheard Elliot talking with Elijah, and so, well..." He let his voice trail off, and it was my turn to clear my throat.

"Yeah. It seems that maybe our timing was good."

"I'm happy for you. He's a good guy."

"And Jeanette's the best." I wasn't kidding. I liked Jeanette a lot. She was talented, sweet, and she fit with Nathaniel well.

I hadn't.

"Anyway, well. This is going to be awkward for a minute, and then we'll get over it." He laughed, and I joined him, feeling a little less awkward than I had before.

"Good. Now don't forget to go over the set list with Elliot, because we want to make sure the festival goes amazingly, but I trust you guys."

"That's good. This is good, Maddie. Very good." He leaned forward as if he wanted to kiss me, just a quick peck as friends, then thought better of it. I grimaced, and he just laughed, shaking his head as he left.

I shook my head as he walked away, going back to see Elijah and Evan, and work on a few more things before the end of the day. My stomach clenched, it felt as if butterflies were doing a little dance inside.

I was going to see Elijah.

This wasn't anything new. I had done this before, but everything just felt different now.

Everything *was* different.

I needed to get a hold of myself. I was at work, I had to stop acting like a schoolgirl with a crush.

People were laughing and joking around on the other side of the event space, as the late-morning wedding with an afternoon reception was winding to a close. I saw Alexis moving from person to person, doing her best to be unseen, and yet always there as the wedding planner.

People were laughing, and two little girls were dancing in their flower girl outfits next to the hill.

I frowned, wondering where their parents were. Nobody else was watching them, and they kept giggling to one another, gently pushing at one another, as if they wanted to see who could roll down the hill. It wasn't a large one, we were in Texas after all, and though this was the hill country, it wasn't as if we had mountains, but it was rocky. We were on limestone, and there were a few cacti at the end of the hill. This wasn't where people normally rolled down for fun, but I didn't think the girls noticed what was down below.

"No, you go."

"No, you." The girls weren't giggling anymore, instead starting to push at each other.

Where were their parents?

Where was anybody?

I moved faster, annoyed with myself for wearing heels. I wasn't on the path anymore, walking on the grass, slightly soft from being watered the night before.

"Is everything okay, girls?" I asked as I got within arm's reach.

The smaller girl, the one with her back to me, turned, her eyes wide, just as the other girl pushed.

The little girl tripped on her own two feet, being pushed a little too violently, and fell. Her little ankle twisted, as she pushed into me.

She didn't mean to, her momentum knocking her right into me. But I staggered back, my heel twisting into the dirt as it got stuck.

Pain radiated up my ankle, and then I was falling.

The little girl was in my arms and we were rolling down the hill.

I clutched her, keeping her head close as I tried to stop us.

She screamed, her voice echoing and searing my ears, as the other girl started laughing at first, before she screamed as well.

I stopped us before we hit the bottom, and I was grateful. Because we were still a few feet away from the cacti, and that was not something I wanted to hit.

The little girl was sobbing, and I sat up, aware that my heel was still up on top of the hill and I was covered in dirt, a few scrapes, but the little girl looked no worse for wear.

In fact, I was pretty sure I had taken the brunt of the roll.

"Jessica!" someone screamed, before the lady who had to be the little girl's mother ran down in her bridesmaid's dress, other people following behind her.

A man in a suit ran even faster, whirling towards me.

"Maddie? What the hell were you thinking?" he asked as I stood up. The little girl went straight to her mother as other people took in the scene, wondering what had happened.

"Excuse me?" I whispered to Elijah, wondering if I'd heard him right.

My elbow hurt, I had blood trickling down my knee, and I was pretty sure I had broken my shoe.

What a great way for a professional to look.

"You could have been hurt. Do you know what could have happened? What the hell were you doing? That was irresponsible. Anything could have happened to you. You could have died."

People quieted as they stared at him. His face was red, a little blotchy, and his eyes were wide with panic.

I knew exactly what he was thinking. Who he was thinking about.

And it wasn't me.

Of course it wasn't me.

Sympathy started to well up, but I didn't have time for that, not right then.

I smiled at him, knowing it was perfectly fake, and exactly what I needed it to be.

"Is Jessica okay?" I asked as I turned to the little girl's mother.

"She is. She only has a slight speck of dirt. You seem to have taken the brunt of it. Thank you. I was trying to run over here to stop the girls as they were fighting. But I didn't make it in time. They ran off, and that's on me. I'm so sorry."

I shook my head, aware that Elijah was glowering at me and others were looking between us, awkwardness settling in.

"I'm just glad she's okay. You guys have some fun. I'll make my way up the hill soon. Try to go get my shoe."

"I've got her shoe," East called out. "And it looks like I'll be putting up a rope to block off access until we figure out what to do about this hill," he grumbled.

No one had fallen down this little hill before. I just had bad luck. But I didn't say that. People began to disperse, for which I was grateful. East gave me a questioning look, as he glanced over at Elijah. I shook my head, fake smile firmly in place.

"I'll come get my shoe in a moment. Okay?"

"If you say so," he grumbled, making off with my shoe.

I rounded on Elijah.

"Okay. Don't ever yell at me like that again."

"What were you thinking?"

"I was thinking I was stopping a fight between little girls. She tripped, and it was a bad set of circumstances. But I'm fine, Elijah."

"You're fucking bleeding. You could have snapped your neck. You could have hit your head on a rock."

"I didn't. You can't take away the hills. You can't stop little girls fighting. You can't stop life. But thank you for making sure I was okay. Thank you for making sure the little girl was okay." I took a deep breath, practically shaking. "But you need to talk to someone if you're going to panic if I bruise my knee. Because I will not have you talk to me like that. Ever."

He growled at me, his eyes narrowing before he whirled and stomped away.

His hands were fisted at his sides, and I didn't know who he was angry at.

Me?

Himself?

Or life.

"Great, Maddie. Good job fucking things up again."

Because I wasn't Joy. She was gone and wasn't coming back, but that's all he had been able to see when I was on the ground. There was no changing that fact. Even if it broke me.

Chapter Eleven

Elijah

"What the hell were you thinking?"

I turned to see East walk towards me —no that wasn't right. He stalked towards me, anger radiating off him with each step.

"What?" I spat, my chest heaving.

Everything was tight inside me and I couldn't catch my breath.

I didn't know what was wrong with me. Why I couldn't focus. But damn it.

Every time that I thought about what could've happened, what had happened, I couldn't breathe.

I rubbed the spot over my chest where it hurt, and realized it was my fucking heart.

I cursed under my breath and began to pace.

"What is wrong with you? Why are you acting like this?"

I looked over at East as my brother narrowed his gaze at me, then reached out and gripped my shoulder. I moved back, not wanting to be touched, but East moved closer again.

Without thinking, I punched him, my fist connecting with East's jaw.

East cursed, his hand going to where I'd hit.

"Seriously?"

I shook out my hand, looked at my already swelling knuckles. "Why is your jaw like granite?"

"Why do you hit like a pussy?"

"You know Eliza would say that pussies take the beating, and we shouldn't be so misogynistic."

East flipped me off. "I don't really want to hear what our sister has to say on that subject. There are lines and I'm not going to cross it. Now, if your hand hurts, it's because you didn't punch correctly. Don't know what your fucking problem is, but Dad taught you better than that. Hell, *we* taught you better. Your wrist was flopping around like a dying fish."

I held back a growl. "That couldn't be further from the truth."

"I don't know."

I looked down at my hand again, then up at my brother. "I fucking hit you."

"Yes, you did. Idiot. What the hell is wrong with you? Why would you hit me?"

"I'm so damn sorry. That was uncalled for." I shook out my hand again, then rolled my shoulders back.

"You're welcome to hit me back. It's only right."

East looked down at his hand, then at my jaw. He narrowed his gaze and I braced myself.

When he sighed and shook his head, I relaxed. "I'll get you later. Probably when I'm the one acting like an idiot."

I tensed again. "Why are you calling me an idiot?"

"You yelled at your girlfriend. Because she tripped. What the fuck is wrong with you?"

And like that, I deflated. My brother was right. I was a damn idiot and deserved whatever came at me.

I moved away, rubbing my hands over my face. "I barely even remember yelling." I paused, my body growing cold as dread and guilt slid over me. "Did I hurt her? Did I touch her?"

East stepped towards me. "Don't you remember?"

I whirled on him, my mouth going dry as I nearly vomited thinking about the what-ifs. "Did. I. Hurt. Her?"

"Her feelings. But no, you didn't touch her. You wouldn't hurt her, Elijah. You overreacted, and we both damn well know why. But no, you didn't physically hurt her. But you left her standing there. She was hurt. Because she fell, and after I came back and handed her that shoe, I came and found you.

"It was like Joy all over again."

I said what was obvious from the start, even if I hadn't realized it until now.

East stared at me long enough I was worried I'd broken him just like I'd broken myself. "I figured out that much. And from what I heard of the last of your conversation with Maddie, she figured it out, too. You want to talk about it?"

I shook my head, a wry smile that had nothing to do with humor sliding onto my face. "What is there to talk about? My girlfriend died. She was hit by a car as I sat there at my table, waiting for her to show up. Waiting with a fucking engagement ring so I could propose to her. So we could spend our lives together. And I hadn't even realized she was dead only a block away. With the music and people talking, I hadn't even heard the impact. Or the screech of tires. I heard none of it. And just now, as soon as I saw Maddie fall and go out of view for just those few seconds, saw the blood on her knee? It's like it all came back."

"It was just an accident. Both things. Yet they were so unalike they're not even in the same realm."

"Don't you think I don't know that? Of course I know that. She fucking tripped. And I fucking overreacted."

East ran a hand through his hair while looking off into the distance. "Yes, you did. And considering I'm the one who usually overreacts and has an anger management problem—according to every single person I've ever spoken to—that's saying something."

I scowled at my brother. He had his own issues, things that we didn't talk about, things I hoped like hell he talked about with somebody. But he wasn't violent. He wasn't the angry man that he liked to portray. At least, I didn't think so.

"You don't have anger management issues. You're just an asshole."

"You're so sweet. I'm here trying to help you, and you call me an asshole."

"It's the truth."

"Maybe, but it's life. All of this is life. Go find her and apologize. We can't bring Joy back. Of course you're going to grieve for the rest of your life, because grief doesn't go away, and we all know that way too well. I have watched my friends get blown up, shot at, and killed in so many ways I can't even name them all. I've had to deal with it even though it's never just dealing. But it's a different form of grief now. And yes, I'm an asshole but it's what I love. It's what makes me happy. Maddie makes you happy. Don't fuck this up. Because if you screw this up, you're not just going to break her, you're going to break yourself, and break this family because she's already part of it. She'll leave, Elijah. And then maybe I'll have to be an asshole to you."

"When did you get so introspective?" I asked, trying to bring some levity into the conversation.

"I have no idea. I'm blaming all the women being added to this family. I used to be able to just growl in a corner, now they're making me speak. I can't just hide in my shack and pretend that you guys aren't there. You all force me into family dinners."

"You forced me into family dinners, too."

The first few after losing Joy had been hell on earth. Everyone had been so careful, as if walking on eggshells would be easier than me sitting at a table trying to pretend I cared. But things were different now.

At least, I thought they were.

"Do you know where she is? If she's even okay? I just left her there."

"You did, but she went to clean herself up. Lark was with her."

"Lark was there?" I asked, confused.

"She was out for a walk and saw some of what happened. I don't know what was said, but they walked off together. I don't even know why she's here."

I raised a brow. "Is there something going on between you and Bethany's best friend?"

"No, she just gets under my skin. I don't know why. But then again, I did mention I was an asshole."

I shook my head, not having the emotional energy to

deal with whatever that was. I pulled out my phone. "I need to find her."

"Do that. And I will go back to what I was doing."

"And what was that?" I asked.

"Everything and nothing. You know me." And on that cryptic note, East left me alone, and while I wanted to follow him, to make sure he was okay, I hung back.

I never knew what was going on with my brother. And that was probably an issue. But I would deal with it. Soon. We all would.

I tried my best to compose myself and knew that I would grovel if needed. Maddie deserved that. She was also right that I needed to talk to someone. And not just East.

I shot a brief email to my therapist hoping I could schedule another session. All my family went to therapy at some point. Maybe just for one session, but we tried. It was one thing that Eliza, our baby sister, had taught us. Talking to someone helped. And if you hid it all, you would break. I would be forever grateful to my baby sister for making me talk to someone.

I passed Naomi, our innkeeper, and she smiled at me. "Everything okay, Elijah?"

I frowned. "Do I not look okay?"

"You look like you've been running your hands through your hair. You usually look a little more put together than that."

I winced and tried to flatten my hair. "Better?"

"You looked fine before, just out of order."

"Do you happen to know where Maddie is?"

She gave me a sweet smile, one that was all knowing, though I had a feeling she didn't know the asshole I had just been. No, the entire property was excited that Maddie and I were dating. I would have to think long and hard about exactly what that meant, and what, if anything, we needed to do about it, but for now, I just needed to find her.

"She's just finishing up a tour."

"Really?" We hadn't been separated that long. She didn't have time to do a complete tour over the grounds with a new group.

"Jay had to go help Evan with something. I'm not quite sure what happened. If it was an emergency, they would've texted you, though. You know them."

"You're right." I picked up my phone and stared at the lack of texts. "Well, seems that they could handle it. She just filled in for the rest of the tour?"

"Yep. She should be done soon though. They were almost finished, but you know Maddie, she just brings happiness to everything that she does."

That was Maddie.

And I was an idiot.

Naomi sobered. "I was going to find you. I'm glad I saw you in the hall."

Worry settled over me. "What's wrong?"

"Nothing's wrong. Per se." She huffed. "Joy's parents

are in the dining room. You know how they come here for dinner sometimes. They're here now, and they asked if you were around. They didn't ask for me to bring you by because they didn't want to bother you. But I thought I'd let you know."

I nodded solemnly and squeezed Naomi's arm. She smiled and tapped my hand in comfort. Naomi and Joy had been friendly, and I knew she missed her as well. It was hard on all of us. "Thanks for letting me know. I'll go say hello."

"You're a good man, Elijah."

"I don't always feel like that, so thank you."

She smiled softly, and headed to go help someone else, while I went to face my past once again in the dining room.

Joy's parents sat at a table near the window, speaking to each other. There wasn't a sense of sadness in the air like there had been the first year or so. Instead, they looked like they were having a lovely night out, enjoying the sunset, and just breathing in one another's company.

Joy's father saw me first, his face brightening. When Joy's mother looked over her shoulder, she waved and gestured towards the table.

I nodded at a few other guests and our wait staff as I headed towards the table. "It's good to see you both."

I kissed Joy's mother's cheek, and then shook her father's hand.

I could see Joy in both of them. She had been the

perfect mix of the two of them, and it didn't hurt to look at them anymore. I figured that was a good thing.

"I didn't know you were coming in tonight. You should have told me."

"It was a spur of the moment thing," Joy's mother said. "Don't worry about it. We were just craving some of that lavender lemon chicken that Kendall does, and so we decided to come out. We didn't mean to take you away from work. I know you must be off soon."

I look down at my watch and nodded. "I'm off now. Though, since I live and breathe here, I don't know if I'm ever actually off duty."

"I'm glad that you're finding new avenues to try to relax," Joy's father put in.

I stiffened as Joy's mother rolled her eyes. "So subtle, Garrett. I mean really, it's like you try to put your foot in your mouth."

"I have no idea what you mean, Linda." They were teasing one another, smiling, but I couldn't speak, couldn't do anything.

"Oh. Um. Well."

"I see that we're not very good about keeping secrets. We heard about you and Maddie. It's hard not to when you're at the grocery store, and you see two of the Wilder brothers' employees talking about how happy they are that you're happy again." Linda looked at me, and I licked my suddenly dry lips.

"Should I say I'm sorry? I feel like I should apologize right now."

She shook her head and gripped my hand. "We love you, Elijah. We come here to eat because we like seeing you. Because we love the food, and we just like being here. This is where Joy was happiest. Her name was her presence. And while we miss her, you don't need to bury yourself in a shroud of what you once were. You're allowed to move on, and I'm so happy that you're doing it with a woman that we adore."

I blinked, an unsettling feeling sliding over me. "I wasn't aware you really knew Maddie."

"We know of her enough. We've been in here often enough to have met her, been on her tours. And we also want you to be happy. If Maddie brings you that happiness, then what more could we want? Joy would want you to be happy."

Suddenly uncomfortable, I was grateful that there was an extra seat at the table. I took it, not wanting to loom over them any longer.

"I don't know what to say to that."

"You don't have to say anything. We all lost Joy. But you should have a future. And we're happy that we can watch it from afar. I know your parents would want you to be happy, so think of us as merely a substitute aunt and uncle who want you happy."

"We'll even slip a $5 bill in your birthday cards," Garrett added, and I laughed.

To anyone else, the situation might have seemed odd. But I liked their family. We spoke to one another about our pain, about who we missed. They didn't hide their grief, or the way that they were healing. They were good people.

But the fact that they seemed so happy about me and Maddie? It floored me.

And it shouldn't have. Because this was who they were, and I was damned happy to have them in my life.

"Thank you. I would love another aunt and uncle."

"Good, because you're family. And we're not letting you out of our lives. And you make sure Maddie knows that too. If things are awkward, she can come to us and we'll talk it out. We don't want things to be weird. Even though they're weird just because I am." She winked as she said it.

I shook my head. "If you're going to be weird, I guess I will be too."

"And I think you should get up and go talk to her."

I froze, blinking. "What?"

"She was just standing in the doorway and then ran off. I hope she's not too worried that you're talking with us." Joy's mother squeezed my hand. "Let her know that we approve. Not that she needs our approval. I don't know. Actually, tell her to come talk to us. Because we want to talk to her." She looked over at her husband. "I'm making this weird."

"I started making it weird, you're just finishing it. It's why I love you."

"I need to go find Maddie." I stood up then, looked at them both. "Thank you. I'll see you soon?"

"Of course. Maybe we'll force Maddie into a dinner and make it awkward all around."

I laughed, said my goodbyes, and tried my best not to run out of the room.

Maddie was in her office, packing up her purse when I got there.

"Maddie," I said.

She smiled up at me, though it was cautious, and I hated that I was the one who made her feel this way. "Hi. I didn't mean to interrupt your dinner. I'm sorry."

I shook my head and moved forward. "No, I'm sorry. That must have been an odd sight to see."

"It's really not. I know you're friends with them. It's good. It really does bring me happiness, the fact that you and Joy's family are so close. It was just a little shocking at first, because I wasn't prepared for it. Even though I didn't need to be prepared for it."

"They know about us."

She pressed her lips together, her face reddening. "Oh. That explained the bright smiles glowing my way and why I ran like an idiot."

I shook my head, leaning forward. "I'm the idiot."

"You know, I'm not really going to argue about that."

I snorted. "They want to do dinner or something. The four of us. They think of themselves as an honorary aunt and uncle because my parents aren't around." She raised her brows. "I know. It's weird, and yet not? We went through something together. We grieved together, and they want me happy. I love them, in a familial way. And I know it's not exactly the norm, or what people think of as something that should happen, but it is. It's my life, and I'm figuring it out."

"I think that's beautiful. And I would love to do dinner with them. I've known them for a while too. They've always been so nice."

"They wanted to let you know that they approve of you, and then felt weird about even having that approval, so it should be a fun dinner."

Maddie just shook her head, laughing this time. "Everything's just so weird."

I reached out and cupped her face. "I'm sorry for over-reacting before. I'm trying to do better. I *will* do better."

"I know why you did it. I just didn't appreciate it."

"I shouldn't have yelled. I shouldn't have done any of that. I do talk to people, you know. I already emailed my therapist for another appointment. But you getting hurt—I guess it was a trigger. I'm learning. Maybe not quick enough, but I'm trying."

She wrapped her arms around my waist, and I held her close.

"I'm learning too. So, we talk to one another. We find out what bugs one another, and we try not to overreact."

I pressed my forehead to hers. "And when we overre-act, we talk to each other to figure out why. Because I'm a Wilder, I'm sometimes an asshole."

She was laughing before I kissed her, and I knew that that was a step.

I just hoped it was enough.

Chapter Twelve

Maddie

"You've been to countless Wilder dinners. You can do this. Nothing is different. Not really. It's just us."

I stared at Elijah in the mirror over my head and scowled. "You're not joking, are you?"

"Why would I be joking? You've done this before. You can do this. It's not going to be any different than a normal dinner with my brothers and Wilder Women."

I blinked at him before I laughed. There wasn't any humor in my laugh either. No, it was more of a panic-stricken "what the hell was I doing" kind of laugh.

"Stop. You're going to be fine. We've done this before."

"No, *we* haven't. You have brought Joy to a Wilder dinner. And that was a big thing. I remember when you brought her and how stressed out she was. And now you're bringing me."

I didn't mean to make the comparison, or to sound as if I were her replacement, but it was out there and I couldn't take it back.

Because I would do anything to bring her back. Even if it meant me walking away and not having what was in my heart. Because she was one of the most generous and amazing people I had ever met, and I missed her. And while that would never change, I stood here, remembering exactly what he had said two years ago while standing in my spot on the hill.

There was this beautiful spot where you could watch the sun rise or set—depending on which direction you looked. It gave me peace and a sense of stability that I didn't have in other places when I felt as if my life was whirling around without me in control.

Elijah had shown up there one day and had yelled at the world for breaking him.

And in that moment, he had vowed never to love again, never to trust in fate or allow himself to feel anything close to what he had felt.

And while some might think it was the dramatics of that moment, and he couldn't have possibly truly meant it, he had. In that moment, he had been telling his truth. That he was done. That he was never going to love again.

The echo of his words still reverberated within me.

I remembered. And while he cared for me, and wanted to make this work—whatever this was—it wasn't love.

He had never said he loved me, and now that the coldness settled in, the reality of my situation taking hold, I wasn't sure he ever would.

And wasn't that a lovely thought to take with me to dinner with his entire family? His family, who would want to know how things were going and what exactly was going on between us. We were all nosy and needed to be in each other's business. It was how we worked.

And I wasn't even truly a Wilder. I was just about to become partners with them. I just slept with one of them. But I wasn't one.

I sobered, the coffee I'd been drinking all day to keep up with my work souring in my stomach.

Elijah turned me, his hands on my shoulders as he stared into my eyes. "What's wrong? We don't have to go. If this is too soon, or too much, we don't have to. We can just stay inside, finish what we started earlier in the shower, and just be. I don't want to rush you. I just thought it would be okay because we've done something like this before. But maybe you're right. Maybe this isn't like before."

He was trying. Trying so hard, and here I was, complicating it and overthinking like I always did.

I needed to live in the moment. I told the girls I was

going to take a chance, just to breathe and to be. So I needed to actually take my words into account.

"I'm fine. A little stressed, mostly because I teased Alexis, Kendall, and Bethany enough, and now they can do it back."

"If it helps, I think Lark will be there. And she's not dating a Wilder as far as I know."

My eyes widened. "As far as you know? What don't you know?" I asked, intrigued.

He shook his head, his hands up in surrender. "Nothing. I just confused myself with my wording," he said with a laugh. "Lark is there because she's probably going to be house hunting soon and is one of us." He paused. "Just like you've always been one of us."

"Now I'm in a whole different sphere. And that's scary."

"A little scary, but we're figuring it out. Right?"

"Of course we are."

"But if you would rather stay home, we can do that."

Home. Such a weird thing. How had we gotten here so quickly? Because we were barely used to touching one another as we were able to over the past couple of weeks.

I needed to stop worrying.

Or maybe I wasn't worrying enough.

"I'm just in my head." And that was the truth. "I would love to just get this over with though."

I needed to live in the moment.

Soon I found myself across the property and at the

free cabin that had a large dining room in it. It was open for the weekend thanks to a cancellation, and rather than trying to scramble to have someone fit into that spot, the Wilders decided to use it for their family dinner. They owned it, so why not. Plus, I loved this little cabin. Though there wasn't anything little about it. It was huge, had six bedrooms, and had the second-greatest view of the entire property.

In my opinion, the best view was of course from Elijah's deck. You could sit there, watch the sunset, drink a glass of wine, and just breathe in the moment.

But I wasn't going to say that where everybody could give me cute little looks and giggle because yes, I was dating Elijah Wilder.

I still wasn't quite sure how that had happened.

"You're here." Alexis threw her arms around me and I laughed.

"You act as if you hadn't actually seen me at work all day."

"Well, now I'm seeing you outside of work. I like it. It's homey."

"I love this cabin. If I could live here I would."

"I think Eli would have a heart attack if he couldn't make money on this place though. Just saying."

"So would I. I'm the CFO over here," Everett added, his arm around Bethany's waist.

She rolled her eyes at her boyfriend, and then waved before turning back to her conversation with Lark.

The Wilders did these dinners perfectly. Kendall usually did the cooking—because she loved it, and didn't trust anybody else in the kitchen, but East helped. It always surprised me that East was such a good cook. And from the way that Lark looked at him, her eyes wide as he brought out a plate of appetizers, I wasn't alone in that.

"I didn't know you cooked." He just grunted at her and went back to the kitchen.

"Sorry about my twin," Everett said with a laugh. "Apparently, he never learned how to talk to human beings."

"I assume that you got all the niceties from the womb."

"They might look identical, but that's about it," Elliot added as he bounced into the room.

I narrowed my eyes at him. "How much coffee have you had?" I asked.

Elliot paused, his eyes widening. "I have no idea what you're talking about."

"I saw him chug the rest of his espresso on the way in," Trace added.

Elliot scowled. "You're not supposed to narc on me."

"I'm the eyes and ears of keeping Bethany safe. Of course, I'm going to notice what you're doing when you walk in."

"Watching how much caffeine I happen to intake, and then ratting me out to my friends and family, is not part of your job."

"I can make it part of his job if you like," Bethany teased.

Trace smiled and it made him look years younger—and damn sexy. Not that I'd say that aloud. "See? It's now written in stone. I don't have an option."

"It is not written," Elliot growled.

I just laughed, loving everybody's interactions.

Maybe Elijah was right, and this wasn't that bad. After all, this felt normal. As if we had done it a thousand times before. And we had.

"Okay now, what kind of wine are you interested in?" Kendall asked as she came forward. "The kids are with the sitter tonight, and while they may be Wilders, I'm kind of happy to not be mommy right now."

"You are just sad that you can't call Evan daddy," Bethany teased.

"No. We are not doing that," Evan snarled. "Do not ruin daddy for me."

"Oh, they've already tried," Eli added, sipping his wine. "It's all they do. Ruin good things."

"Us?" Bethany asked, her eyes wide and her lips twitching. "I would never."

"I don't trust that innocent face," Everett said with a laugh.

"So disheartening. But I don't mind it. I love you."

"I'm just glad that she didn't call him daddy," Elijah whispered into my ear, and I held back a shiver.

And then it seemed that all eyes were on us. I held in a

curse as I picked out my wine, a deep red blend that was perfect for the meal Kendall made. Elijah picked the same.

"When did this happen?" Trace asked, looking between us. "I mean, I knew you guys were close, but this is nice. Pretty cool."

"I thought you were supposed to be all-knowing?" Elliot teased.

"Hey, it's still new. We're taking bets on exactly what's going to happen next though," Alexis teased.

"What bets?" I asked, before I held up my hand. "You know what? I don't want to know. As someone who was on the other side of this, I know better."

"Serves you right," Kendall teased.

"I have no idea what you're talking about. I'm innocent in all of this."

Elijah grinned at me, before he inhaled the bouquet of the wine and took a sip.

I did the same, letting the Wilder wine settle on my tongue. This felt normal, something I was good at.

"Am I supposed to be smelling my wine?" Trace asked.

"I can get you a beer," East put in.

Beside Trace, Elliot laughed. "We do serve beer here. And liquor. You do not have to have wine if you don't want to."

"Sacrilege," Elijah teased.

"It's true. When you have a bunch of Wilder Wines owners here, you have to drink it."

"And soon you'll be one of the Wilder Wines' owners," Alexis added, beaming.

My heart skipped and I swallowed. "It's a little weird though, don't you think?"

"I think it's about damn time," Kendall added, holding up her glass. "To the future partner of Wilder Retreat and Winery."

Everybody held up their glass and I blushed, ducking. "I didn't want to be the center of attention," I grumbled.

"We're proud of you. Sue us." Elijah leaned down and kissed my temple, and I blushed even more as everybody cheered.

"You're not helping."

He held out his glass to me, and I took a sip. "I'm not trying to help."

I went all warm and gooey inside, and everything felt weird.

"Well, I figured that you might feel a little weird today," Everett put in as he leaned against Bethany.

"Really? Am I that obvious?" I asked with a laugh.

"Not really, but we love you. So, rather than this be about the fact that you're here with Elijah and everything's all high-school girl high-pitched in our heads when we're thinking about it, we have an announcement to make."

I froze, my eyes wide, as Bethany held out her hand.

A very shiny diamond sat on her ring finger, and everyone broke out into cheers and exclamations at once.

I set my wine glass down and threw myself at Bethany. She hugged me tightly, laughing.

"I'm so happy for you."

"Thank you! He asked last night. We thought today would be a good time to break the news to you guys. And you're not in the spotlight."

She whispered as she said it, and I held back tears, holding one of my new best friends.

"You're going to be a Wilder. That's crazy," I said as I stepped back.

Everyone began to talk at once, with East coming in with chilled bottles of champagne.

I raised a brow at him, and he shrugged. "He's my twin."

I didn't know if that meant that East had been told to prepare the champagne, or if he just knew because of some twin psychic thing. With East, I didn't ask questions.

"Bethany Wilder, I kind of like the name," Eli added, his voice that same soothing deep growl as always.

"Professionally, I will still go by Bethany Cole. But when I sign things, and it's just us, I'm going to be Bethany Cole Wilder. I can't really get rid of the Cole too easily, but I want to be all wild with you guys. It's great, isn't it? A built-in massive family."

"To the Wilders!" Lark said, not a hint of joking in her tone. She meant it, and so did I. I held up my glass with hers, as everybody cheered the new happily engaged couple.

Soon there was talk of weddings, and the fact that the paparazzi and the rest of the world would be interested in this wedding. I knew we could handle it, because we could handle anything, but I mostly sat back and watched as the family came together, as the next stage of their lives started to be planned and was glorious in every way possible.

Elijah sat by Everett, talking about something. I smiled over at him. He winked before going back to his brother, and I pressed my lips together, worried. I didn't know what he wanted. I didn't think this moment would be in our future. Not with that promise he had vowed. He had told me plainly.

I couldn't love him. Not like I had before. And that was something I needed to remember.

If I didn't etch that into my heart now, I would shatter when everything broke. When we went back to the realities of working together, of finding out that maybe this was as far as we ever went.

I would have to let this be enough.

I knew his promises. The ones he always kept.

Elijah didn't lie. Not even to himself.

Chapter Thirteen

Elijah

For the countless time in several weeks, I woke up with a soft and curvy woman in my arms. Not quite snoring, but those deep breaths that told me she was sleeping.

Considering we'd stayed up far too late the night before finishing what we started that morning before coffee, I didn't blame her for sleeping as hard as she was. If anything, it just made me grin and think about exactly how much we had enjoyed our evening.

She moaned slightly, arching into me, and I placed my hand on her hip, keeping her steady.

While I wanted nothing more than to slide right into

her—and the way that my hard cock pressed against her ass making that far too easy for both of us—I knew we had other things to accomplish that morning. Things that didn't have anything to do with us touching one another.

I sighed, pressing a kiss to her shoulder.

I was glad she hadn't woken up from my dream. From the way I had called out her name.

Because I wasn't sure what I would have said if she asked me what was wrong.

The dream had been like normal. Me sitting at the table, a ring burning a hole in my pocket. I had watched the candle flicker on the table, the wax melting and gathering in pools as time wore on. I heard the sirens pass but hadn't thought anything of it.

But unlike in real life, I stood up and made my way outside.

I walked up the block to see what had happened, to see the horror unfold as blood pooled on the ground and people screamed.

I made my way to where her short dark hair splayed on the ground.

The way her eyes looked up at me glassy, unseeing.

I'd had this dream countless times before, and it shouldn't have been anything new.

Only, it wasn't Joy lying there.

It was Maddie.

I screamed and begged the world to bring her back.

But, just like with Joy, the fates hadn't deemed my screams worthy.

And then I had woken up, dream Maddie dead in my arms, and the real Maddie warm and supple as she pushed into me, keeping me steady even in my nightmares.

"If you keep kissing my shoulder like that, we're not going to be able to get to work today. And it's kind of an important day."

I grinned and kissed her shoulder again before I quickly pushed all thoughts of my nightmare away. "I suppose we should get ready for the festival."

"It's early enough, and you have a meeting with your brothers first. And I have to go work on a few things. I want to get my workout in, too, because it'll calm me down."

She turned in my arms and I kissed her softly, the dream fading away completely from my mind, as if it had never been there.

"I think we can find a different way to work out."

"Perfect," she whispered.

And then I didn't let myself think. If only for the moment.

The road to the small meadow needed to be patched up. The gravel a little too loud, the potholes getting bigger with each passing storm. We were hitting the rainy season, the one where it was either a drought, or flash floods all over the place, but today was a beautiful day.

And that was a good thing, considering we had the festival that night, and we needed a good showing. We needed to make sure that we didn't screw up this chance of ours. Our company needed it. Our family needed it.

Maddie needed it.

It was so odd to think that she'd become so important to me so quickly. Or maybe it wasn't that odd. And maybe it wasn't that quickly.

I shrugged out of my reverie and pulled into the small lot off the beaten path. Only people who knew this spot existed would park here. Most people didn't even know about this location where you could watch the sunrise. But I did. And so did Joy's family.

I got out of my car, the crunch of gravel underneath my boots echoing within the meadow's absence of sound.

A few birds chirped as the breeze slid through the large oaks around us.

But it wasn't too loud. After all, it was still early enough that I wasn't even sure all of my family was awake.

Maddie was at work, prepping her part for the festival, and I would be there soon. I just needed to do this one thing, instead of my normal morning jog or hike.

My fist clenched around the flowers I picked up from the grocery store on my way here. Not the prettiest, not even fully bloomed, and still somehow slightly wilted, but they were something. I hated to come here empty-handed.

Joy's family had taken care of her grave and funeral, and I knew her mother came out weekly to clean any debris, and to talk with other mourners. She was open about her grief, and shared it with anyone who wanted to know. But she didn't force it on others.

Some people just wanted to talk about what hurt. And some people just wanted to talk about the person that they loved. The person they had lost.

I wasn't sure who I was in that regard, but I stood here in front of the small grave and swallowed hard.

We were in the middle of a drought, even with some of the torrential rains that hit us in the evenings, so the wildflowers that grew over the grave sites were a welcome sight. They were native plants, much like we had on our land. Things that could thrive in this climate.

I knocked a fallen leaf from the top of her headstone, and set down the flowers.

Joy had been in her twenties when she died. A year younger than me at the time.

She'd had her whole world in front of her, a world I had wanted to experience with her, and it hadn't been enough.

"I just wanted to say I loved you."

I swallowed, my voice breaking as I tried to formulate the words I needed.

"I'm not good at this, you know. The others thought I was. They always thought I was good at words, making those connections. But I'm not. You brought that out of me. Made me smile when I felt like I was so lost."

My fingers gently pressed against her name etched into the stone. "I don't come often to see you. Because I see you when the sun rises, when others speak of you. I loved you. I did. And the man I was would have been with you forever, Joy."

The wind tickled my face, and it felt as if someone caressed me, even though I knew it wasn't true.

Joy wasn't here. And she hadn't been for a long while.

"I'm a different man now, Joy. I'm not that person that loved you. I would have always stayed true. I would have always been yours. But I'm not him."

I swallowed hard, the words coming out gruff. "I love her. I love Maddie. You know I was always faithful. I didn't love her like this before. We joked that you had seen my crush on her, before we dated, and I had laughed it off, but I never lied. There wasn't a moment during our time together where I ever wanted her. Not in that way. Because I was faithful. But I love her now. And I hope you would be happy for me."

I was rambling now. "I need to tell her. And I have a feeling you would have been the first person to tell me that."

I smiled, imagining her rolling her eyes at me. "I don't want to be the man that becomes a shade in his grief, but I remember the promise that I made. That I would never love like this again. And what a fucking liar that made me." I let out a rough chuckle. "But I'm so fucking scared. What if she leaves? What if she realizes that there's a whole world out there beyond us Wilders? She deserves it. Just like you fucking did. And look what happened? The world took you away from me. They took you away from everything. What if it happens with her? What would I do without her?"

I huffed out a breath, a single tear falling as I gripped the flowers against the ground. "I don't even know how I'm supposed to function without you, but I do. And I'm finding different ways to thrive, and it's because of her. But anything could take her in a moment. And I'm so afraid if I let myself fall completely, if I trust that, I'll be hurt all over again. And I'm not ready for that."

I loved Maddie, and I wasn't ready. And I didn't know when I would be.

And that was a fucking shame.

"Goodbye, Joy. I loved you." I pressed my fingers to my lips, then to the stone, before I stood up and made my way back to my car.

The drive was easy this time, maybe because a different weight was on my shoulders than before. But it didn't matter. We had things to do, a festival to host, and our world to embrace.

As I pulled in, my phone chimed and I looked down at the email notification, my lips twitching.

It was like she always knew.

From: Maddie

To: Elijah

Subject: Is it hot in here?

Actually, I do have a question about the heat. I feel like the heat is on in the lobby of the winery, and now I'm afraid I'm going to sweat out all of the festival-goers. When you get back will you come and see? Your brothers should be in soon.

And since we're talking about hot in here, I'm going to say something that is very bad for our HR.

I groaned as I read the text, then laughed.

Thankfully it was our personal emails, not our work email addresses, but I just rolled my eyes.

We were crossing every single line that we could in any other world, but this was ours.

And she made me smile.

I slid my phone back in my pocket and headed into the winery area.

Everybody was doing their best to set up for our part of the festival, beginning today. We had two and a half days to wine and dine the Texas elite.

I moved towards Maddie, seeing her like a whirlwind, and scowled as I saw she wasn't alone.

Clint Dustin stood there, laughing at something she

said, and I wanted to hurl myself at the brewery master, wondering why the hell he was here so early.

Maddie saw me, her eyes brightening. "There you are. Clint was here early to say hi, and to get the lay of the land. Apparently, he wants to poach."

I scowled, glaring at the man. "What exactly do you want to poach?"

I didn't mean for my voice to sound so deep, so menacing, but fuck it.

The man raised a brow, looked over at Maddie, and snorted. "I told you he was going to think I meant you. I meant your setup here. We're looking to expand a bit on the eatery part, and I know you're already working with Roy for your brewery needs, but if your guests want to go north rather than east, we should talk. We could be good partners." He winked at Maddie. "But not partners how this man thinks. I swear, he looks like he's ready to rip my head off."

I scowled between the two of them. "Are you done making fun of me now?"

"Maybe." Maddie rolled her eyes. "Come on, we have to set up. And Clint actually does have a proposal for us."

My brows rose. "Indeed?"

"You sound so British and proper right now," Clint said with a laugh. "My brothers and I even typed one up, but that's for later. Now, you're going to shine like a star and make everybody regret not putting you guys on the list years ago. I always fucking hated the Dodges and their resort. So it's good to see you here."

"Well, that makes me happy," Maddie said with a smile. "Though I will say there is a Dodge around here. He's our lawyer."

Clint shrugged. "LJ, I liked. Not so much the others."

Anger spiraled in me, as I remembered exactly why I hated LJ's family. "Oh, we hate them. And we have good reasons to."

The other man's eyes darkened. "So I heard. And that's the last I'm going to bring up on that subject. Let's talk about good things. And, if you need an extra pair of hands, I'll help."

I looked around, honestly surprised he was even offering. "We're good actually. We've been prepping for this."

"Hell yeah you have. Everything looks great. And I like the whole family aspect of it. Reminds me of ours."

We spoke for a few more minutes, before Maddie was called off to work on something else, and I went off to work with Evan. We had a thousand things to do, but this was what we were good at.

Wine, family, and entertaining.

When the organizers of the festival showed up, the Wilder brothers were out in full force. We'd even dolled-up the kids, even though they were still decently small, and the festival owners lapped that up. Alexis was her dreamy self, looking gorgeous and professional as she and Eli walked around with a couple of the organizers and a few other winery owners. Kendall shone as our chef, and honest to God made food that tasted as if it came from the heavens themselves. I saw more than a few guests who were there just to eat for the festival literally moan and tilt their heads back whenever they bit into one of the canapés.

We had gone for San Antonio's best. A little bit of Tex-Mex, a little bit of barbecue, and a whole lot of wine. We made damn good food.

We had set up so everybody could see the different aspects of the Wilders.

We had actual staying guests who had already planned to be there before we got in the festival lineup. Meaning people were already there staying in the cabins and were welcome to join for the food and wine festival part. We also had people coming into the city just for this, and locals who wanted to taste-test some of our food and wine.

We even caused a bit of a ruckus as Bethany and Everett walked in, the newly engaged pair grinning as Bethany signed autographs and posed for photos. But the best part was that she had on the Wilder Retreat and Winery shirt and was helping just like the rest of the family. She wasn't a celebrity here; she was a Wilder-To-Be, and helping with the festival which just elevated us.

Maddie shone like a beacon. Everywhere she went, people fell at their feet for her. She smiled, made sure everybody was happy, and signed on more wine club members and potential buyers than I thought possible. Even if we were never on this festival circuit again, though I hoped to hell we were, we were going to hit a new level because of this day. And I knew it was mostly thanks to Maddie. Yes, we Wilder brothers knew what the fuck we were doing now, but Maddie got us here. And Maddie was going to push us further.

When a woman with dark hair came up to Maddie and hugged her tightly, the two laughing with one another, I frowned, wondering where I had seen her before.

East was at my side, scowling as usual but, honestly, it looked a bit less than before. Maybe that was his happy face.

"Who is that speaking with Maddie?" I asked.

East looked over to where I pointed and shrugged. "That would be Ivy. Of Ivy Wines."

I froze, remembering the winery that had wanted to take her from us. Maddie was about to be partner, as we had put off signing everything and going through the paperwork until after the festival because of the timing, and yet this was the woman that wanted to take her away. Who had given her an offer to spread her wings.

"I want to hate her for being here. For trying to take Maddie away from us."

East let out a short laugh that grated. There was something wrong with my brother, but he was the worst of us when it came to letting others in. "You could still end up hating her. I mean, all of us could. Because Maddie hasn't signed on the dotted line yet. She could still go. So don't fuck this up."

I scowled at my brother. "Seriously?"

"What? You guys have done an amazing job today. And you know I don't give out praise lightly."

I snorted, knowing that that was an understatement from my brother. "I'm not going to fuck this up." Though it sounded like I was going to do exactly that.

"I need to go fix something. Don't screw this up with Maddie. I like the way you two are together. And I don't like many things."

"What's broken?" I asked, ignoring the last part of his statement. Mostly. because I had no idea what to do with it when it came to East.

"Nothing. But I feel the need to fix something. So let me do it." He scowled like he usually did and stormed off.

Maddie still spoke to Ivy. I just shook my head and moved on to speak with one of the other festival organizers. People were eating and drinking, and it was just day one. We had a thousand more things to do, but this was it. This was the big chance for the Wilders. For my family.

And yet I could only think of Maddie.

Chapter Fourteen

Elijah

As the final day of the festival wound down, I made my way through the throngs of people, smiling, laughing, and doing my best to wine and dine each of them, all the while trying desperately not to make it look like I was running towards the woman in the corner.

Maddie stood there with her hair in a complicated knot on the top of her head, a bright smile, and brighter eyes—though I could see the exhaustion in them. Every single person that worked for the Wilders, including the Wilders ourselves, was exhausted. I was pretty sure all of us were going to sleep for days once this was over, but I didn't want to say anything about how the event had gone until later. But soon, we would leave the people to themselves, and I would head with Maddie back to my place.

Each night of the festival we had slept side by side, exhausted, our hands barely touching in my king bed. It wasn't that I didn't want to cuddle with her. Damn it, it was the only thing I wanted to do. But that would have required excess energy that neither of us had.

Last night we had slept with our clothes on, barely rousing to shower and try to look as if we knew what we were doing the next day.

"Wilder," a deep voice said from my side. I turned, even though he could have been talking to nearly a dozen people in this room.

Even my sister and her family had come down from Colorado to visit, and to see how things had gone. I figured that was a good sign, since getting all of us together when there were children to consider made things a little more complicated.

"Jeff, it's good to see you," I said as I held out my hand to the organizer of this whole thing. He grinned, then laughed, that deep booming laugh hopefully meaning good things. I never knew when it came to him.

I hoped that laugh meant that he was happy, and we hadn't completely screwed up. But for all I knew, this was the beginning of the end. I needed to stop thinking so pessimistically, but it wasn't always easy.

"I just wanted to tell you how great this has been. I

know this was last minute, while most places have had nearly a year to prepare, and you only had a few weeks. But you guys blew this out of the park. All I can say is, we can't wait to see you next year." He winked as he said it, slammed his big hand on my back a few times before he adjusted his Stetson, and made his way over to another set of people.

Eli came to my side, bumping into my shoulder. "Did I hear that right?"

I just blinked, trying to comprehend exactly what had just happened. "I think, I think the big man of this festival, Stetson and six-six of muscle, just said that we're in next year."

Eli grinned, as Elliot came over out of nowhere, a tray of champagne in his hand. "Well, good thing I already poured champagne into the flutes." He winked as all of my brothers came to my side, taking a glass. Even East, though he was scowling more than usual and I didn't know why.

"To the Wilders."

"To you pulling this off."

"To Maddie."

"And to all of us."

"Fuck yeah."

I pressed my glass to theirs before I drank half of it in one go. "Well, I know we shouldn't celebrate too soon, and we have more to do, but fuck yeah," I agreed.

I met Maddie's gaze over the groups of people, and she raised a brow in question.

As if he knew exactly what I needed, Eli handed me another glass of champagne, then exchanged mine for a full one.

"I'll just finish this," Elliot said as he tossed the rest back. "Go schmooze with your girl."

And with that, my little brother walked away, talking a mile a minute with someone else.

"How much champagne has he had?" I asked.

Eli laughed. "Not that much. Honestly, I think that was his first drink. He's just excited. Hell, you're even making me excited. And that's saying something."

"It's a little scary, honestly," I said with a laugh, before I nudged his shoulder and made my way over to Maddie.

I held out the glass of champagne, and she took it willingly.

"Sorry it took me forever to get over here. You are always surrounded by people."

"They love Wilder Wines. Now, while I'm really sad that I didn't get a photo of all of you Wilders standing together looking amazing, can you tell me what that was about?"

I pressed my lips to hers, then held out my glass.

She smiled at me but gave me a curious look. "Elijah?"

"Jeffrey just pretty much confirmed that they'll be seeing us next year."

Her eyes widened and she beamed, tossing her champagne back, setting the glass down next to her, and throwing her arms over my shoulders.

I laughed and bobbled my glass slightly before I kissed the top of her head, drained my own glass, and set it down. "We are going to break those one of these days."

"Maybe, but it'll be worth it."

She just shook her head, staring at me. "Are you sure? You weren't just hearing things? How much wine have you had?"

I shook my head and kissed her again. "I'm sure. Eli heard it too."

"That's amazing." She shook her head, held me close. "I know we have to go talk with other people and be all sociable for the next hour or two, but I'm so proud of you. So proud of all of these Wilders. You guys have changed so much since you showed up here, all fresh out of the military and growly and wondering what the hell you were doing. Now look at you."

I met her gaze and wanted to tell her right then how important she was to me. But then I remembered Ivy Wines. I remembered the fact that others wanted her. That she deserved the best.

And she could leave.

So I just kissed her gently and moved back. "I guess we should go and be sociable."

"I guess so." She paused. "By the way, since we're being open and honest, I got three more job offers today."

I froze, panic settling in as my heart began to race. It took all my self-control to sound calm and collected as I replied. "Really?"

"You should see your face. I promise, it was all in good faith. Since they don't know that I have plans on staying here, they were good offers. For nearly what I'm doing now and to try to get their wineries up and going beyond the start-up phase."

"Kind of poor taste for them to offer while I'm standing here."

I heard the growl and disappointment in my tone, and so did she. "It's how the world works, and I said thank you for the offers, but I'm fine where I'm at."

"Good."

But I didn't miss the way she said fine. As if it wasn't more than that.

I knew things would change, but damn it, I wasn't ready to hear any of it.

I squeezed her hands and gestured towards the groups of people. "Let's go do what you're best at."

"*We*. We're best at it. We're damn good at it, considering that we just got an invitation for next year." She went to her toes, kissed my chin, and left me standing there, laughing as somebody asked her a question. She was so good at what she did. No wonder people wanted her. No wonder they wanted to poach her from us.

Yes, we had offered her partner and she had accepted. But she could still leave at any moment.

Because we Wilders wouldn't make her stay if there was something better for her out there. Even if we were better with her here.

Even if I was better for her being here.

It took four more hours before we could leave. Four hours of me trying not to panic at the thought of her leaving.

But I needed to give her a reason to stay. The Wilders had already, so now it was my turn. And I wasn't going to fail.

Our staff helped clean up as much as they could after everybody left, and I knew we would have more to do in the morning. We were still an operating retreat. And we had to feed and entertain our guests in the morning.

Naomi, our innkeeper, was working double-time to make sure everybody who was there not only for the festival, but also those with regular reservations, were happy and well cared for. Every single person here was giving their all.

But now it was late, and it was time to go home.

At least to my home.

"I know we've been spending a lot of time at your place, but it's so convenient."

I rolled my eyes. "I'm so glad that me being convenient is why you're sleeping here."

She snorted, and I hoped she didn't hear the odd note in my tone. I didn't like feeling so unsure about my own self-esteem. So I wasn't going to let myself.

It was weird. Because that wasn't me. I was usually better than this.

"The sex is good too. But I assumed you knew that."

My dick pressed against my zipper. "That's good to know."

"Of course, though with the fact that your bed is so nice and convenient here, it does make me a bit of a workaholic. I can just roll out of bed and make my way over to the winery."

"It's why we have the golf cart. So I can get there faster."

"You just like driving a golf cart."

I shrugged, undoing my tie. "It was something that I wanted as a kid, and I got it. Shocking."

"Spoiled, more like."

"Maybe, but it's what I'm good at."

"I think you're good at a few more things." She practically purred as she said it, and I groaned.

She moved towards me, prowling like a cat. I froze, letting her do what she willed. Because whatever she willed meant that I was going to be a very happy man.

She licked her lips and slid her hands up my chest.

"Are you in the mood for a game of Yahtzee?" I asked, teasing.

"I don't think I've ever played Yahtzee in my life," she said, shaking her head.

"It's fun. When we were younger we used to play it on military bases because it would be the only thing left in TLF. And then when I was in Afghanistan, they had it at one of the bunks."

She tilted her head, studying my face. "Are you okay

talking about those things?" Her voice had softened and the part of me who would have walked away from this conversation stayed.

I brushed her hair back from her face, studying her gaze.

"I am. I didn't see the same things that my brothers did. My job meant I was in a different place. Not quite as in the thick of it."

And while I used to have guilt over the fact that my brothers were all in more dangerous situations than me, I didn't feel that any longer. Not when we had all gone through our own hells, and sometimes I just had to be grateful for what I did have. Because I had learned first-hand that you could lose it all without even knowing.

"I'm glad that you all talk to each other, to go through things."

"We didn't always. Everett hid a lot of shit from us. Hell, so did Evan."

"And what about East? And Elliot? I don't know about them. They don't talk."

"They don't." I swallowed hard, picturing my brothers' faces when I had first seen them after so long being apart.

"I don't know exactly what they went through, and I know they're talking to some people, but not us. But it's at least something. And while I wasn't in the thick of it, neither was my sister, and she was still hurt by everything that happened over there. It's those we leave behind that are left to pick up the pieces sometimes. And I don't think we realized that until we weren't surrounded by every-thing else."

She tilted her head, studying my face. "Well, you're home now. All of you. And you have each other. For that, I'm grateful."

I combed my fingers through her hair, grateful that she had taken the updo down so I could. "I'm glad I'm here too. Now, you had your hands on my chest earlier. Do you mind finishing what you started?" I asked, my voice low.

She slid her hands down to my hips and tugged on my belt.

"Oh, I think I can do that."

It was soft at first, a gentle kiss here, a gentle caress there.

And then we were stripping each other, laughing as we tumbled into bed, naked and already panting.

My hand slid between her legs, playing with her deli-cate folds as my thumb found her clit. She arched into me, pressing her body along mine as I began to explore her with my fingers. She rode my hand, her pussy clenching around my fingers, I rubbed her clit in gentle circles as I pressed my mouth to hers, needing her taste.

She came on my hand, her body writhing as she rotated her hips. I moved so I was kneeling between her legs and licked my fingers clean as she watched before I put my mouth right on her cunt.

She shook, letting out a gasp as I licked her, her body still coming down from her first orgasm.

She was wet, pretty and pink, and I wanted every inch of her.

I spread her again, licking, going lower as I teased her asshole with my finger.

She shivered and I dipped my finger inside, before going back to her pussy. When I slid my fingers over her, teasing her back entrance again, she froze, before I used her wetness to make it a little easier.

I breached her softly, watching as she shook, just one finger going to the knuckle.

Her eyes widened as I slid my finger out and went back to licking at her pussy, making her come once again.

Her whole body shook as I moved over her and into her in one strong thrust.

I pressed her knee up to her ear, going deeper, as her eyes opened wide.

"No warning?" she asked, gasping.

"I'm going to fuck you hard into this bed and then you're going to remember exactly who I am. Got me?"

"I always know who you are, Elijah."

I captured her mouth with mine, and I kissed her and I fucked her hard into the bed like I promised.

I moved her other leg up, both knees at her ears, thrilled she was so damn flexible.

I kept moving, fucking her harder and harder until both of us were shaking, and then I rolled us to the side.

One of her legs was around my hip, the other pressed

to mine, as we moved against one another, side by side, raw and passionate and exactly how we liked it.

I didn't want to think of the future, didn't want to think of tomorrow.

I didn't care in that moment if there were no tomorrows. I just needed today. Tonight.

When she came again, I held her close, and I knew letting her go would kill me.

But watching her walk away would do something even worse.

But I couldn't clip her wings, couldn't force her to stay.

I just held her close. And tried to remember that we had tonight. And that had to be enough.

I should have known that it wasn't enough. That the dreams would come.

This time she fell from the same hill where I had first told the world I would never love again.

She fell, and kept falling, screaming my name. I reached forward, trying to catch her, but I couldn't.

She lay dead on the rocks, blood pooling around her head, staring wide-eyed at me.

And then the dream changed and we were drowning, water filling my lungs as I reached for her. I pulled up, gasping for air as I breached the surface, but she wasn't there.

I looked down through the water, at the storm, and she reached up at me, and I could hear her scream. It didn't matter that it made no sense, that I shouldn't be able to hear her from underwater, but I heard her scream my name, to yell at me and shame me for not saving her.

And then the dream changed again and fire licked at us, and then there was nothing, just her screaming. Accusing.

Because the world would keep taking from me. It always did.

The world would take her away. Or she would walk away.

And I would be left behind.

Again.

Chapter Fifteen

Maddie

Rain poured outside the front windows and I looked down at my phone, noticing the new weather alert.

A flash flood warning, a severe thunderstorm warning, and rain.

Lightning lit up the sky, and I shivered.

"Well, my weather app isn't lying. Seriously though. This is a lot of rain."

I was just talking to myself, but I was a little worried about Elijah driving in this weather.

My phone didn't alert with a text, but I knew he would be on his way soon.

But I also didn't want him to get in a car accident or veer off the road in the rain.

I shivered, this time a little harder than before, remembering exactly why he hated the rain and cars, and how things had changed for him once before.

I shot off a text to him, hoping that he hadn't left yet. And hoping that he wouldn't check his phone if he was already on the road.

ME

> The rain looks bad. Maybe you should stay home until it gets better. I don't know about the roads near the creek. Miss you. I'll see you soon if it's safe.

I hit send and hoped that it would have to be good enough.

I didn't want him to worry about me, and while I wanted to see him, I also didn't want him to get hurt in the process.

I was still exhausted and exhilarated over all that we'd done the past few weeks. We had accomplished so much, and the Wilders' businesses were going to do amazing things.

And on Monday the lawyers would officially sign me into the partnership.

It was scary, a whole lot of money, and a whole lot of freaking out, but it was going to be worth it.

I might be dating a Wilder, but I was also going to be part of the Wilders in every other sense.

It was a huge thing, and part of me didn't think I was ready.

And the other part of me felt as if I had been moving towards this forever.

He didn't text back right away, and so I had to assume he was already on the road.

That didn't make me feel all warm and fuzzy, but from what I could tell, the rain seemed to be dying down.

That was going to have to do, and I had soup to finish. I gasped and practically ran to the kitchen—how had I forgotten the vegetables?—and opened the oven. The tomatoes, peppers, onions, and garlic still sat in my uncovered dutch oven, roasting away.

This was a recipe of Kendall's, a roasted tomato soup that was supposed to go with the bread she had made that morning. I wasn't willing to try to make my own bread, not right now. But maybe one day I would be good enough at it. Or maybe not.

I snorted, closed the oven door, and hoped I wouldn't spray tomatoes all over the kitchen once I had to mash them with the immersion blender. That, of course, I had borrowed from East, because I didn't actually own one.

I wasn't the greatest cook, but I was learning. Hopefully I wouldn't burn down my house in the process.

I went to check my reflection in the mirror, worried that all that steam in my face had made me look like a frizzled-out hedgehog, but I looked fine.

This was just Elijah. He had seen me at my worst and

my best. We had been dating for a few weeks now, our relationship completely changing, and yet not. That's what worried me. Everything had changed.

Everything had come together so quickly, but now that we were taking a moment to pause, to reflect, to just breathe after the festival, and figure out who we were, we could just sit back for a moment.

I was about to become partner. I had a future with the Wilders, and Wilder Wines was going to make a splash. We had already done so, and the first write-ups about the festival were already being showcased on different blogs. People were even making social media videos for us, and we didn't even need to do ads.

We were making something of ourselves as a company.

I was doing what I had always wanted to do, find something that pushed me, that made me thrive, and remember that I could do things like this.

And now I was here with Elijah, and that was one more step.

We had time to take things slow, to do something together that wasn't just a quick dinner and a sweet and sexy time in bed, before then heading back to work.

It was time to just *be*.

I had come to realize that in the weeks we had been together we had fallen into a rhythm, and I didn't want to take that for granted.

My phone buzzed, and I quickly picked it up, hoping it was a text from Elijah, instead it was just my alarm, my tomatoes having apparently been cooked all the way through.

I didn't know if I quite believed that, but Kendall said I needed to follow the instructions exactly, so I would.

I got out my potholders, opened the oven, tried not to burn my eyelashes off, and pulled out the vegetables. I nearly dropped the pot, and I winced, using my knee to close the oven door, as I set the heavy dutch oven filled with the yummy smells of what would soon be soup on top of the stove.

The olive oil on the bottom bubbled, the garlic smelled completely roasted and was a little brown on the edges. The onions had begun to wilt, and the tomatoes had that wrinkly skin texture, so I counted that as a win. At least it looked like what Kendall said the recipe should be.

I should have asked for pictures. Pictures would've helped.

My phone buzzed again, and I cursed myself for hitting snooze instead of off on the alarm, so I turned that off and plugged in the immersion blender, hoping I didn't make a mess.

"Well, here's to hopefully not having to take a shower later when I throw tomato all over myself."

I hit the button once, and it whirled, splashing tomato purée all over the back of the stove.

I turned it off and groaned.

"Okay, a little slower. A little more prayer."

I put a paper towel over the edge of the pot and hoped that would work.

My phone buzzed one more time and I looked down, thankful that I didn't have the immersion blender on yet.

Maybe Elijah would be better at that, because I sure as hell didn't know what I was doing.

I set the blender down, ignoring the way that it rolled almost off the counter.

I was going to break something, and hopefully it wasn't my foot.

I quickly answered the phone before the person on the other end of the line hung up.

"Hey, Lark. How are you?"

The other woman laughed slightly at something someone else was saying, before she finally answered. "I'm doing great. Sorry for calling you out of the blue. I know cold calls can be scary. I know we're much more of a texting generation."

I snorted, leaned against the stove, then I winced and stood back up, remembering that the stove was hot and I might burn myself. I hadn't burned the soup yet, but we weren't done.

"No, it's okay. I'm making a mess in the kitchen and phone calls are great. I'm on the phone all the time."

"Sometimes I just need the sound of a person, and my hands hurt after playing with the guitar all day, so I wasn't in the mood to text."

I winced though she couldn't see me. "I can only imagine."

"It's not fun for sure. But I wanted to call you because with my schedule and Bethany's, traveling is a little hard right now."

"I don't know how you guys make so much time for each other as it is."

"It's not easy but we make do. However, I wanted to try to do a girls' weekend. I know that there's going to be an engagement party with the Wilders and everybody, and then of course there's the bridal shower and everything that normally comes with that. I don't know exactly what Bethany wants, but I would like to at least try maybe a girls' weekend just for her. We could have it at the Wilders, or somewhere else. Somewhere we can find privacy. But I'd love to plan it with you and the girls. I probably should have done a group text, but like I said, texting and I aren't fun right now."

I grinned. "That sounds wonderful. We can totally set it up. And maybe we'll do a video call or something so we can all get on at the same time. Is this a surprise for Bethany?"

"Not a surprise. Mostly because trying to get our schedules to work means she doesn't get to be surprised much. But you were the first person I thought of when it came to planning, even though Alexis is the wedding planner. But you're the one who just did the festival, so I figured it'd be nice to celebrate that too. Maybe a milestone for everyone since we haven't really been able to just sit down and enjoy ourselves."

"You did just win a Grammy. Did we celebrate that?" I teased. It still surprised me every day that I was friends with Lark and Bethany. This didn't seem like my life, then again, I was dating the man of my dreams, so maybe I was dreaming.

"We didn't celebrate, but I always feel weird."

"I feel weird about celebrating accomplishments too, but you should. And I think a girls' weekend or trip could work. Let's set up the actual video chat, so that way we save your hands, and we can see all our faces."

"Even though most of you guys can be in the same room."

"Maybe, or we'll do it separately so we could all be in our own homes. Who knows? We'll make a plan."

We talked for a few more minutes, the smell of garlic and tomatoes filling my nose and reminding me that I had to finish making dinner, before we hung up, and I grinned.

Elijah was on his way to my house for once, rather than going to his, the weather was getting better, not as much rain, and things were looking up. The winery was soaring, my friends were living thrilling lives, and I was about to relax with the man that I loved.

Yes, I loved him. And not the same type of love that I had when it was just a crush. Because I had loved the man he had been, when I had been a different woman. Now, who I was had fallen in love with who he was all over in a completely different way.

I loved the way that he cared for his family, the way that he put his all into what he did. I loved how he made me laugh, how he made me smile.

I just loved being with him.

I still didn't know what would happen next, or if what I wanted was the same thing he did. But I had to hope it would be enough. That what he had said on that hill wasn't his truth. Maybe he would finally come to terms with the fact that he was allowed to love.

Or maybe I was thinking too hard and wanting something that couldn't happen. But I didn't want to think about that.

We had both changed, and I wanted to believe that he loved me back.

However, I told myself that it was time to take a step back, and just breathe in the moment when it came to Elijah. So, I was going to do that.

Because damn it, thinking too hard, and worrying about the future when I didn't even feel like I was always living in the present wasn't going to help anybody.

My phone buzzed again, this time with the alert sound that echoed sharply in the kitchen. I frowned and saw the flash flood warning blinking over my screen.

Just when I thought the rain had stopped, it came down again, this time in such a downpour, I couldn't even see through my front window.

I turned to the side, trying to see the creek that I could usually barely see over the hill, and I froze.

"Oh my God."

Martha stood out in the rain, her hands on her mouth as she looked forward.

I dropped everything and ran, the rain hitting hard, the wind shaking my house. It didn't matter that there was lightning, or that I wasn't even wearing shoes.

Because the creek had overfilled, like it always did, and my house might be slightly above hill, but her house wasn't.

And she was standing lost in the rain, and I could barely catch my breath.

"Martha! Come here, get out of the rain."

"But the storm is here. And I want to play on the beach. I just want to see the whales."

She continued to speak in a singsong manner as I ran to her.

Then it sounded like a train was barreling towards us and I tripped, looking behind me.

It wasn't a tornado, no, but it was something just as bad.

Water hit us, harsh and unrelenting. I reached out for her, but she just let the water sweep her away. I tried to stay on my feet, the water quickly at my knees, then at my shoulders.

When they say flash floods hit Texas, it wasn't just a little trickle. It was a storm. A surge of water that came out of nowhere, even if you thought you were safe. They say to *turn around, don't drown,* because you don't know how deep the water is, but this wasn't that. This was a flood out of nowhere on the plains because the water couldn't be absorbed down into the dry packed dirt quick enough.

This happened in a desert, in a drought, and this happened in Texas every season. It had happened to this creek before, but never when I had been standing outside, never when the water went above my head, my feet slipping as I pushed up from the ground, hoping I knew where the bottom was, where the air was.

Rain continued to pour, the wind whirling, as I slammed my knee into a rock. I cursed, shaking, as I reached Martha. She thrashed, and then looked at me, her eyes suddenly cognizant.

"Maddie. Oh, Maddie, I'm so sorry."

"It's okay," I lied, my voice choked with fear. "Let's get back."

We held onto one of the oaks that was still standing as the water pushed at us. I pulled at her, grateful that she wasn't fighting me anymore, as we made it closer and closer to the edge.

This wasn't a river with an obvious direction to get out of the current, this was an unending flood that didn't make any sense.

It could be over in an instant, or it could go on for eons, I just didn't know.

A branch snapped and hit me across the face. I could

feel the blood starting to trickle from my nose as Martha screamed out, the branch slashing her as well.

But I had to ignore the pain, had to ignore hers, as we got to the edge.

"Maddie! Maddie!"

I looked up at the sound of Elijah's roar as he came towards us, barreling through the edge of the water.

The flood had begun to recede slightly, and though we had been thrown hundreds of feet away, I kept moving towards high ground.

Elijah barreled forward, and pulled at me, but I shook my head. "Her, help her."

He met my gaze and nodded tightly, as he pulled my neighbor into his arms, and began to carry her out of the water. I knew in that moment that he'd broken something inside to do that. To help her over helping me.

He couldn't lose me, but I wasn't about to be lost.

I held on to the tree, trying to get up, as another wave hit me, knocking me under the water.

I swallowed way too much water, dirt, and whatever else was mixed in as I tried to move up, but I couldn't.

Panic set in, and I moved underneath the water, trying to break the surface, the current too strong. I reached up, gripping something, a tree? I didn't know. But I pulled myself up, gasping for air, as I choked, my eyes stinging, my throat burning, as Elijah's screams echoed throughout the night.

I couldn't focus, couldn't breathe, and then he was

there, pulling me out of the water, as other people were shouting, sirens blaring.

I didn't know what had happened, how long I had been there, I just lay in his arms as he pulled me to the side, holding me close.

Other people were moving about, the water receding even as the rain kept coming down.

I saw Martha underneath a blanket, a paramedic with her. He spoke to her in soft tones that I could barely hear over the rain. But Elijah was holding me, and I tried to figure out what had just happened.

I had nearly died. Nearly been swept away by the creek that was near my home of many years.

I couldn't read Elijah's eyes when my gaze met his. Not in my panic, not in my fear.

I had almost died, but Elijah held me, and I hoped that I would wake up from this nightmare.

Chapter Sixteen

Elijah

"Elijah? Elijah?"

I turn to see East standing there, staring at me. "Hmm?"

How long had I been staring at the closed door, at my closed door, wanting to go inside, but not knowing if I was even fucking allowed to. I kept hearing her screams, and then nothing. The silence as the water took her under again. All I could see was another tree branch floating past, the raging current increasing with each passing moment.

I couldn't even catch my breath as I pushed back the panic, the fear.

I needed to go inside, but East was talking to me, and I couldn't hear him, just a whisper, then a scream, and then nothing.

"Elijah," East grunted again, squeezing my shoulder.

I turned to him, eyes wide. "She could have died. I almost lost her."

Just like I'd lost Joy.

I slammed my thoughts down on that, because I couldn't think like that. If I did, it would all be over, though maybe that's what I should do.

No, no. Not now. Not ever.

"Okay, just breathe. You're okay."

I whirled on him. "How can you say that? She could have died out there."

"But she didn't. She didn't. You saved her. And she saved her neighbor. She's fine. You're fine. But I'm going to need you to breathe, because you're not doing that right now, and it's starting to freak me the fuck out."

"I'm sorry you're fucking stressed out. I'm sorry if that is hurting your delicate sensibilities." I sighed as soon as I finished speaking and shook my head. "Sorry. You don't deserve that."

"No, I don't. But you don't deserve what just happened, just like she doesn't. But at least you're talking. At least you have some form of reaction. I was getting fucking worried because you weren't saying anything, you were just standing there, and I was afraid you were frozen. And I wasn't talking about temperature."

"I need to go inside."

"Then go. They're not keeping you out. They're keeping us out, but we're just here to make sure she's okay. To make sure you're okay."

East kept talking, and I knew Eli and the others were behind me, all talking about what had happened.

The storm had hit us hard, now it was gone. Clear skies, because that was Texas storms. It was dark now, so you could see a few stars, but I wasn't going to look up. I couldn't even focus on anything.

The authorities had taken Maddie's neighbor away, and her family would be there to take care of her soon. She would be fine, a few cuts and scrapes, though I knew she had to be exhausted after everything that had happened.

Her house had been damaged in the flood, but Maddie's was fine. She hadn't even lost power.

I remember walking through the house when I had first gotten there, confused why the back door was open, a pot of tomatoes and garlic and things on the stove top, music playing, the lights on, and a bottle of pinot noir open and breathing on the counter.

It didn't make any sense to me, until I heard her scream and I ran, not even thinking about what I was doing.

I would never be able to get the image of her head going underwater the first time out of my mind. I thought she was gone. Gone and never coming back.

Just like Joy. Just like my parents. Just like the countless men and women who had died over the time I was enlisted.

They all left, and they never came back. I had been so afraid that Maddie wouldn't either.

I wasn't sure when I had moved, but I had my hand on the doorknob and walked inside, grateful that Maddie was in bed, covered in a blanket, and smiling at something that Kendall said.

My sister-in-law looked at me, gave me a sad smile, and said goodbye to Maddie before she walked towards me.

"We'll get out of your hair. The kids are with Elliot and Alexis, and I guess we should make sure that everything's okay there. The storm should be done for the night. So just get some rest."

She squeezed my hand and kissed my cheeks, but I didn't feel it. Didn't feel anything.

I went to Maddie's side as my family said goodbye from behind me and closed the door. "Elijah. I'm glad you changed into something warmer. Do you want to get into bed?"

She sounded so small, so soft.

"I don't want to disturb you. You need your rest."

She frowned at me, a small frown, a little nudge of her eyebrows. "I just want to be with you, Elijah. I'm okay. It was scary for sure. But you got us out. Both of us."

I sat down on the edge of the bed and gripped her hand. Her skin was so soft, her body warm.

That was good because she had been so cold before. So damn cold.

"I'm really okay. You don't need to stress out."

I just blinked at her. "You don't want me to stress out? You could have died out there. How else am I supposed to react? You could have died, and there would've been nothing I could have done."

"But you were there. And I'm okay. It was a freak accident."

Her face was pale, and I let out a harsh laugh. "I know about freak accidents. You're okay, but you should get some rest."

"Okay. I could use some rest. But why don't you just lie down with me. Please?"

I shook my head. "No, baby. You should sleep."

"I want you to just hold me. Okay? I know it's scary. I was scared. But I'm okay now. And so are you."

"I'm just glad that you're here. That you're safe. And that you're warm."

She sat up, slid her fingers along my cheekbone. This didn't seem real. As if she weren't here. As if I had truly lost her.

"Will you hold me? I just want to feel. I know that's cliché, like something you see in movies, but maybe it's there for a reason. I just want you to hold me. I was so scared. But then you were there. And it's weird to think that I knew you would be, but I knew."

I didn't want to hear her tell me that she knew I would

help. That she thought I could save her. I did—this time. But what if I hadn't been there? What if I had been later? What if I had been sitting at a table thinking about the future when my world ended?

Just like before.

But I didn't have answers to that. And I didn't want to think about it.

I leaned forward and kissed her softly. She wrapped her arms around my shoulders as I lay down next to her, holding her close, continuing to kiss her, just needing to feel, like she said.

I couldn't feel anything else, not right then.

And when the kissing turned to more, I didn't care that it was probably too soon, that we both needed a moment to breathe, because we both needed to *feel*.

I let her strip me out of my clothes, and I did the same to her. I gently rubbed my thumb along her nipple, watching the way that it pebbled underneath my gaze. And when I slid my fingers between her legs, gently bringing her to orgasm, her wetness coating my skin, I let that be a moment of feeling. A moment of something that I couldn't quite name because there was nothing else within me.

It was as if I were watching this from the outside, begging myself to feel, begging myself to do anything but what I knew had to happen in order to protect her.

I didn't want her to be hurt, I couldn't watch her disappear into the water again and drown, or have any other earth-shattering instance break her. I wouldn't let that happen, and I didn't want to tempt fate any more than I already had. I hovered over her while she kissed me softly, reaching between us to place me at her entrance. I slid inside her, slowly, oh so slowly, until I was balls deep, her pussy clenching around me. I swallowed her gasp, covering her mouth with mine as I moved, neither of us speaking, as there were no words left between us. I continued to kiss her, make love to her, do anything to show her how I felt without using the words.

The capriciousness of fate seemed to be cruel, because fate had almost taken her from me. Life had thrown its hat in the ring and laughed at us when we thought we could have everything.

She'd almost died, and here I was, holding her too close, knowing this could be an ending.

We were like moths to the flame, but the flame burned. It took everything away and it left nothing but ashes and embers in its wake.

And that's what I had to remember.

I had promised myself I would never love again, that I would never let myself be hurt like that again, and yet it felt like someone had gouged out my intestines, my insides, everything, until I was a hollow husk with nothing left for her. There had been nothing left for Maddie before this, and yet I had lied to her. I had lied and told her that she could have me, but there was nothing left to give.

Carrie Ann Ryan

I didn't deserve her, she didn't deserve the shell of a man who thought he could possibly love.

I didn't. I couldn't. There was nothing left of me.

I lost myself in my thoughts and in the motions. She came again, crying softly as she held me, whispering something I didn't want to hear. Something I couldn't hear. Something that would make it real, and I couldn't allow this to be real. I followed her, coming and knowing that this was an ending in every sense of the word.

I let her fall asleep, and I knew I would hate myself in the morning.

More than I already did.

Because everything I touched turned to ash, and I couldn't let that happen to her.

I couldn't let that be Maddie.

The dreams came again, but this time they weren't made up, they were memories. Maddie screamed for me, shouted as she reached for me through the water, yet I couldn't reach her.

I couldn't hold her.

There was nothing for me to do other than watch her head go beneath the water, as the rain pounded into my flesh. I bled where I stood as the water choked me, but Maddie was gone. Screaming as the world took her again and again and again.

She stood in front of me, a pale imitation of who she had once been, and she shouted at me.

And then Joy was there, screaming.

"You knew this would happen. Everything you touch dies. You are nothing. We'll all die because of you. Don't you see? You're the common denominator. You're the one who does this. It doesn't matter if you think it's fate. It's *you*. Do you want to feel this again? This horrendous pain that never goes away? Because you will. Because Maddie will leave. She'll walk away when she realizes she can have something better. Or death will find her just like it found me. Do you want to be that man again? Do you want to be nothing?"

I turned from Joy as Maddie fell back into the water, but she didn't fight to come up, instead she drifted down to the bottom, and I couldn't reach her, I couldn't save her.

———

Light hit my eyes as I struggled to wake up, Maddie pressed against me.

Sometime in the night we'd became entangled with each other again, wrapped up in sheets, both of us holding the other.

I could barely hold in what I needed to do. What would be best for her. She deserved more than what I could give. And it had taken me far too long to realize that.

When I rolled groggily out of bed, a hollow ache slid

into my stomach and I swallowed down the bile before I went to change.

Maddie sat in bed, her hair wild around her face as she stared at me. "Are you going into work today?" she asked, her voice soft, a cautious smile on her face.

I'd put that smile on her face. Or perhaps it was what had happened the previous night. I'd be the one to make that smile drop. It was the only way to keep her safe. I could have loved her, if I had that in me. But I didn't. And she deserved more.

So fucking much more.

"There are a few things I have to do. You can stay as long as you want. I'll see you around."

"Why do you sound like that?" she asked, and I knew my voice was cold, deadened. There was nothing left.

Because if I let it, I would break open and Maddie would be gone.

Joy was dead, and Maddie would be next.

I just knew it. If I stayed with Maddie, she would die. It didn't matter that it made no sense, that life didn't work out that way, I knew it. And she deserved more than me.

"I can't do this," I whispered. I hadn't meant to say that out loud, hadn't meant to have this conversation while she lay naked in my bed.

Maybe if she hated me, this would be easier. She would find a way to grow, to be who she needed to be, without me. I shouldn't have taken that step with her. I shouldn't have done any of this. But I was a selfish bastard, and I deserved anything she threw at me. Anything.

"What? Go to work? You don't have to. You heard your brothers. You have the day off today if you want. I mean, flash floods happen, but not usually when we're in it." She was trying to tease about this, to joke around as if she hadn't almost died, while I could barely suck in air.

"You were right before. It's too complicated with work. As is evidenced by last night, I don't handle things well, and I just think it'd be better if we went our separate ways. If we went back to how we were before the festival. You will make a great partner, will be great with the Wilders, but I feel like I'm clouding everything, so I think we should end it."

She blinked at me before her mouth parted and she slid the sheet more firmly around her, as if she needed to protect herself.

And she did. From me.

She needed to.

"No. What on earth are you talking about?"

"You need time to rest. I should go."

"No, you don't put this on me. You're breaking up with me? Right now. When I'm naked in your bed?"

"Maddie."

"Tell me the truth, Elijah. You're just ending it with some complicated thing that makes no sense?"

"If that's the way that you want to look at it."

"Be honest."

"I...need to go."

All the blood drained from her face, and her hands dropped the sheet, but my gaze didn't leave her eyes. I knew that if I didn't end this here, she would hate me more later. She might hate me now, but she would despise me later if I stayed with her.

"I can't lose someone again. I love you, but I can't love you. I'm sorry."

I turned on my heel and I left, knowing that I was running away from the most important thing in my life, doing it because I was a fucking coward. But it didn't matter.

And the first time I told her I loved her, it was because I was leaving.

I scrambled outside and bent over and threw up everything that had been in my stomach spilling on the ground in front of me. I heaved and I heaved.

And when there was nothing else, I wiped my face and went to work.

It was the only thing I could do, because nothing was making sense. And Maddie needed to be safe.

And she wouldn't be with me.

Chapter Seventeen

Maddie

I felt as if I were standing in front of the abyss, wondering when the end would come. I didn't want to be dramatic; I didn't want to wonder what could have been. I had made my own choices, and now I was supposed to do something about them.

After Elijah had abruptly changed the dynamic of what I'd thought we were, I had quietly gotten dressed and held back my tears. I still didn't know how I was able to do that. To not cry or throw things or wonder why everything had changed instantly.

Oh, I had a feeling I knew why. He was afraid.

Because I had almost died, and he was so afraid that he had to push me away. But I was worth more than that.

I have to be worth more than that.

I had taken my meager belongings from his house, emptying the drawer he had given me.

He had given me a damn drawer. Because he wanted me to be part of his life. At least, that's what it sounded like, and then he'd taken it all away, snatched it out of the air as if it meant nothing.

My hands shook, but I promised myself I was okay. That I wasn't going to panic or throw things.

I left, grateful that I had the day off.

I would have had it off anyway, because of the festival and needing to relax according to the Wilders.

My throat tightened at that thought.

And then, after the flood, everyone had told me to stay home and recuperate, and check for any damage at my house. There wasn't, my house had been perfectly safe, even though the flood had washed out the farmhouse down the road and damaged my neighbor's home.

It had taken so much from us, had damaged so much, and it was only just the beginning.

I didn't know exactly what would happen next with Martha, but I had called to check on her, and she and I had talked for a few moments that morning.

I hadn't let on that I was dying inside, that nothing else felt the same. Because it shouldn't matter.

In an instant, Elijah had walked away. It had been too

much for him, and he had spewed words that made no sense. I still wasn't sure exactly what I was supposed to do with that. Was I supposed to fight harder? To scream in the face of his blankness and iciness?

All I did was fight, to try and be worth something, and I wasn't.

He looked at me and he saw Joy. And it had taken me far too long to realize the truth in that. I hadn't wanted to be her replacement, but in the end that's all I was. I had lied to myself long enough.

My phone rang and I paused, looking down at it. I didn't want to talk to my friends, or anyone at work. I just wanted to wallow at home and pretend that my life wasn't falling apart. That, come Monday, I would have to sign papers because I had promised that I would continue my life with these people.

And they would look at me with pity and know that Elijah had dumped me.

That I had let myself fall once again for a man who didn't want me.

It didn't matter that he *loved* me, but he didn't want to. And that hurt more than anything.

Fuck Elijah Montgomery. I was done.

I frowned at the readout on my phone and answered, swallowing the bile in my throat, but knowing I needed to be strong. I was Maddie Swift. I was better than this. I was stronger than this. And if I kept telling myself that, I would eventually believe it.

"Hi, Ivy," I said, hoping my voice didn't sound as falsely bright and cheery to her as it did to me.

No one knew that Elijah had left me, had broken me. And I didn't think most outside of our small area knew that I'd almost died the day before. I didn't want to become the center of a news cycle or anything like that.

"Hi, Maddie. I was just checking in, and to say that I so loved being invited to the festival. You guys were one of my favorite stops."

I grinned and leaned against the kitchen counter. My dutch oven was currently in the sink, soaking after being left overnight with food in it, and I didn't want to think about the grossness of that.

I needed to make something for myself to eat, but I wasn't in the mood to do anything. And that was a problem. Because I didn't want my life to be controlled by the pain that I currently felt. I just didn't know what to do about it.

"Only one of the best? I guess we're failing."

Ivy laughed. "No, but I'm trying to be nice and not sound like I'm sucking up to you."

"Why would you need to suck up to me? You all did pretty damn well yourselves."

"You're right. We did. Although we would have done better with you," she said with a laugh.

Guilt twisted at me, even as something else rekindled, something I didn't want to think about.

"I'm calling to say thank you for the lovely stop on the

festival, and that congratulations are in order. You and Wilder Wines are doing a fantastic job. I am so glad that you are going to soar with them. And yes, I hate the fact that you're not going to be working with us, but maybe we'll figure out a fun event to do as a partnership. Because I love your brain, I love what you think up, and I love Wilder Wines, too. So, even though you might be competition in some respects, in the end we're all wine family, and I'm just happy for you. One woman to another, I'm so damn proud of you."

This time tears did prick at the corners of my eyes and I swallowed hard, wondering why that almost sent me over the edge.

I couldn't just stand there, not speaking, not knowing what to say. Because I had nothing. I had decided to stay here because it was a good opportunity, and because I didn't want to leave my friends or the life I was building. But I had also stayed for Elijah. And he didn't want to want me.

Why did I hate myself so much?

"Maddie? Are you okay? What's wrong?"

I didn't know Ivy that well. Only enough to know that she would have been a great boss, but we weren't friends, and I wasn't ready to talk about why I felt like my heart was breaking into a thousand different pieces.

"I, um...well, things might be changing. I can't get into it, but I might not be taking the partnership after all."

I didn't even realize I was saying the words, I didn't

realize I was even thinking them, until they were already out.

"Oh. Maddie. I'm so sorry to hear that. I know you don't know me that well, but if you want to talk about it—"

"Not really. It's a business thing," I lied.

I had a feeling she knew I was lying, but she was gracious enough not to mention it.

"We haven't filled the position yet here. So take some time and let us know. We have a couple of weeks until we make a final decision. And, well, we just want you to be happy. And to kick ass. Just let us know."

I wiped away my tears, annoyed that I was even letting them fall.

"Thank you. Sorry for feeling like a rubber band right now, but I think the festival just put everything into perspective. I had to put it first, because it was a commitment I made, and now I need to figure out what comes next. Thank you," I said, doing my best to hold back everything that fought inside me. After we said our goodbyes, I wondered if I had just made a mistake, or was I finally fixing one?

Before I could ask myself anything more than that though, my doorbell rang, more than once, and then someone was beating down the door. Alarm shot through me as I made my way to the front of my house and looked out the window.

Alexis and Kendall stood there, anger on their faces, and I knew they somehow knew. I didn't know who told them, but there was no hiding it now. I opened the door with a resigned sigh as two of my best friends glared at me.

"Why didn't you call us?" Kendall stared at me.

I let out a hollow laugh and thankfully didn't start crying. Instead, anger slammed into me, and I moved back, holding my hand out. "Come on in. Enjoy my misery."

Alexis leaned forward, gripping my hand. "What happened?"

"The same thing that always happens. I got dumped. I've gotten good at it recently."

And that was the crux of it all. In the past two years, I had been dumped by not one, not two, but four people.

"Maybe I'm the problem. That's me. The fucking problem."

"Stop quoting Taylor Swift lyrics, and don't blame yourself," Kendall snapped. "What happened?"

"He broke up with me. Just like that. I think we both knew it would happen. We were only trying after all. To see if our friendship could be something more, and it couldn't. Because I'm me."

"Stop it. You don't think that."

I just snorted. "Of course, I think that. What else am I supposed to think?"

He didn't want to love me.

I told them exactly what had happened and the anger in their eyes flared. They reached out to hold me, to hug me, but I held up my hands, knowing that if I did that, if I let them, I would break. And I couldn't break just then.

"I'm fine. Really. There's no need to worry. I just need a minute to breathe, and then I won't talk about it anymore."

"Maybe you do need to talk about it," Alexis said.

I threw my hands in the air. "Talk about what? The fact that I should have known that I would just be second place to Joy? And that's fine. She was an amazing person, our friend. I loved her too. And she's gone, and there's no taking that back. She got hit by a fucking car because of a storm. I almost died because of a storm—of course he's going to compare them. But I'm done. I'm done being second best. I'm done being so worried that I'm going to say something to push him away. An actual literal act of God scared him, and he went away. I don't want to do this anymore. I don't want to pretend that I'm not good enough anymore."

And as the tears started to fall this time, they held me and I didn't push them away.

"I think I'm going to take the job with Ivy Wines," I whispered.

They froze. "What? You can't. You're part of the Wilders," Alexis whispered, and then she cursed. Kendall started growling next to me.

It was a very good imitation of her husband, but that was the problem. Her husband was a Wilder. They were all Wilders.

"I love you guys. I love that place, but I don't want to do this anymore. I don't want to pretend that I'm okay when I'm not. I was ready to move on because I needed a challenge. I needed to show my worth and know my worth. And I don't think I can do that when every time that I see him, I'm going to remember what I lost. What I could have had if I had been good enough."

"Don't. You don't get to think that. If you need to leave to go find something in your profession that is a better fit, then I will support you," Kendall snapped, as Alexis' jaw tightened, before she nodded in agreement.

"But you don't get to think that Elijah is part of your worth. You will always have a home with us. Fuck him. I'm sorry, I love my brother-in-law, but he doesn't get to decide this. He doesn't get to decide if you are worth love. If you need a job that thrills you, I get it. Hello, I came to work with my ex-husband because I needed that. We sometimes have to make sacrifices to find the job that we want. If we're lucky enough to find one. And I know you could do amazing things here, but if every time that you are at work, you feel like it's Elijah's place, then do it. But, we're not going to let you leave us completely. Fuck Elijah. You're family too."

They held me, I let them wipe my tears, and I knew that this was probably the thing that I needed to do. This was the step that I had to take.

When they finally left, after Kendall force-fed me something delicious she made in my kitchen—I hadn't even realized I had all those ingredients, but she was a master chef for a reason—I sat on my couch, considering my job offers.

Multiple people wanted me. And the Wilders would give me a reference. Because even if Elijah didn't want to love me, he was a businessman first. He wouldn't shame me in my career.

He would just shame me everywhere else.

A small part of me knew I should fight for him. To be understanding.

But I didn't want to be. I wanted someone to put me first. And maybe that was selfish, and I understood why he did it. But that didn't mean I had to go along with it.

My doorbell rang again and I frowned, wiping away my tears, knowing my face was red and blotchy.

When I opened the door, I froze, that half-hope that it was Elijah shriveling.

Because he'd left me.

Elijah had left me, and he wasn't at my door.

Instead, Clint Dustin stood there, his Stetson in his hand, a brow raised.

"Hey. I heard about the incident yesterday. Just wanted to check that you were okay."

"How do you know where I live?" I asked.

"It's listed on your return address for the Christmas letter you sent once. And I realize that sounds kind of stalkery, but I just wanted to check that you're okay. I did come by Wilder Wines today, but they said that you were at home resting."

He met my gaze and I shrugged.

"Oh. I'd say come in, but I'm not really ready for company."

He nodded and looked around the place. "You want to talk about it?"

I froze. "I've no idea what you're talking about."

"I saw Elijah, Maddie. I saw his face. He fucked up somehow, didn't he?"

Just hearing his name made me want to scream, cry, and lash out, even as I still wondered how he was feeling. I wanted Elijah to feel as bad as I did, but I didn't want him to be hurt.

I felt as if I were a doormat in this moment. But was I? No. I was just someone who couldn't help who she loved.

"I'm sorry, but I don't know you. Not well enough for that."

"Well, you don't have to say anything, but I feel like I should say something."

"Because you have a say in what's going on in my life?" I asked, knowing the bitterness in my voice didn't sound like me.

He let out a hollow laugh. "You know, if you don't want to stay here, we'd love to have you at our place, but that's not why I'm here."

I blinked. "What? Is this a job offer?"

"From what I hear, you don't need a job offer from us. You're the belle of the ball and they all want you. But you know what? I let someone I love walk away because I was too damn scared to fight."

"Excuse me?" I asked, my voice chilly. I didn't like the fact that he could see right through me, that this man seemed to know so much even though I hadn't told him anything.

"I hear things. Or, at least, I heard Elijah grumbling under his breath, looking as broken as you do. But damn it, I walked away, and I don't want to watch someone that I admire and respect make the same mistake."

I laughed hollowly and knew there was no reason to be secretive. I didn't care anymore.

"Elijah left me. So I don't really think that I'm the one that's doing the walking away."

"I walked away because I didn't fight. Don't be me. And that's enough of me stepping my foot into shit that has nothing to do with me. Be well. And if you really do need a job, we've got you."

I shook my head as he got in his truck, wondering what had just happened.

Because, apparently, I hadn't fought for Elijah.

But he didn't fight for me either. He had walked away because he'd gotten scared, and apparently I was supposed to beg?

No. I was going to put myself first. Somehow. Maybe I'd stay with the Wilders, maybe I'd go somewhere else, but I was going to put myself first for once. I had taken a risk on him. I had taken a risk and lost. I had put a man and my feelings for the Wilders ahead of my own growth.

And I was done.

As I locked the door, I slid to my knees and wept. I was strong. I was powerful. And I wouldn't let this break me. But first, I would let myself feel. Because it was about damn time.

Chapter Eighteen

Elijah

I had fucked up. Not just a little bit, but to the point that there was no fixing this. I didn't deserve it to be fixed, I deserved to have my ass kicked.

But in the hours since I had seen Maddie last, I didn't know what I was supposed to do.

If I would've just let myself think, maybe it wouldn't be like this, but there was no going back now. I had hurt her. I deserved her wrath, and I deserved any pain that I got.

Because I hated myself more than she could ever hate me.

"What did you do?" East asked, and I turned to see my brother glowering at me.

I rubbed my hand over my face and pushed back my hair. "What are you talking about?"

"You looked like you just had an all-night bender. And while I know yesterday was traumatizing for many reasons, you didn't have a drink as far as I know. So, why are you here? Why aren't you at home with Maddie making sure that she's okay and knows that she's loved? Why the hell did I see her driving like a bat out of hell to get away from this place?"

I rubbed my hand over my face. "So, she left?"

"Yes. You didn't know that? What did you do?"

"I would like to know that as well," Elliot said as he walked into the room, Everett, Evan, and Eli behind him.

I looked at all my brothers and didn't know what else to say. I told them the truth.

"I fucked up."

"Did you grovel? Groveling is always good," Evan suggested.

"Tell us what you did first, then we'll tell you how to grovel correctly," Eli added.

"Or do we have to kick your ass first?" Everett asked, studying my face as he tilted his head.

"I broke up with her."

East moved forward, slamming his fist into my jaw.

It was so quick, I didn't even realize it until I staggered back and put my hand on the wall to steady myself.

Everyone started yelling at once, and I rubbed my jaw, blinking at my brother.

"You just hit me?"

"Of course, I hit you. I told you I would. You hurt her, you hurt this family, I beat the shit out of you. Now put your hands up and fight me back, before I kick your fucking ass."

"You don't talk much, but when you do, there's goodness that comes out of it," Elliot put in, and rolled his eyes at East's glare.

"Don't start with me or I'll hit you too."

"Should we talk about your penchant for using your fists instead of words?" Elliot asked.

"One brother's trauma at a time, please," Eli growled as he came forward. He pressed his finger into my chest, glaring daggers at me. "You broke up with her? The morning after she almost died, you broke it off with her. Please don't tell me it was for her own good, because if you say that I won't have to kick your ass, because my wife is going to do it for me."

"Damn straight, my wife will help," Evan added.

"My fiancée will hold him down and make sure he really gets it in his kidneys," Everett spat.

"It was Joy all over again. Don't you see that? Everyone that I love dies."

"We're standing here, aren't we?" Elliot asked.

"And you all almost died. You were shot, blown up, went through so much shit. Eliza was hurt, everything just keeps happening, and I'm done. I don't want to watch my family die anymore."

"That makes absolutely no sense," East snapped. "We're standing here. Maddie was standing there. She risked her life to save someone else, and you went right after her. What were we going to do if the water had swept you away? If you had died? Did you think about that? No. All you did was dive into yourself like you always do and hide what you're truly feeling. You could have died too. Are we supposed to walk away because we're too scared of getting hurt again?"

"The woman that I loved died, and now Maddie almost did."

"If you call yourself the common denominator, I'm going to send you back to school, you dumb shit," Eli growled.

"Threats aren't helping," Elliot said quietly, even though he had threatened me already. "I know you're hurting. But you need to face that fear. We have fear in everything that we do every day. Both of those things were freak accidents. Our jobs before this put ourselves in danger, but we're not there anymore. We're not there, and we're never going back. But there are dangers in everyday life, situations that are unfair, and fate doesn't care what we want sometimes. But you can't run from it. Don't you see that? If you are so scared to see her hurt, why are you hurting her?"

I threw my hands up in the air, as all my brothers stared at me.

"I know it was a mistake. I knew as soon as I said the words it was a fucking mistake, but I can't take them back. I don't deserve to have her back. I hurt her because I was a fucking coward. Because every time I close my eyes, even before the storm, I see her dead. I see Joy dead, I see her dead, and it's too much. I don't know how to keep going when all I do is see different ways for her to die. It makes no fucking sense. I know it doesn't make sense. I know I should have stayed and I should have talked to her about it, but every time I dream, I see her drowning. Or on fire, or getting hit by a car, or lightning, or whatever. I literally dream of her choking and I can't save her and I can't get through the crowd while she's dying. Or she slips on a puddle of wine and a glass shard from the broken wine glass cuts her carotid artery. Literally, all of that fills my dreams, and I can't stop it. I don't know what's wrong with me."

I rubbed my hands over my face. Eli came forward and squeezed my shoulder. "What we're going to do is what we should have done a while ago."

I looked up at him, my body shaking, bile filling my throat.

"What is that?"

"We're going to go talk to someone. As a family. We let you do this on your own, and you were doing okay, but something triggered this, so we're going to go talk with someone. You're going to talk with us, and then you're going to find Maddie. Because you need to fix this. She is everything. You know that. And yes, we're all fucked up. None of us are undamaged, or not emotionally scarred in some way, but we will talk it out."

"Your fears aren't unfounded," Everett put in. "But if they're controlling the narrative, controlling everything that you do, then there's an issue there."

I blinked. "Did your therapist literally just speak through your mouth?" I asked, as East snorted.

"The amount of hell we went through, you know Eliza forced us all into therapy. You apparently haven't been going enough. Or maybe you have, and you can't get through it. We're going to talk it out. And if that doesn't work, I'll beat it out of you."

"Again, this is probably something we should talk about in therapy," Elliot added.

"We're going to talk it out," Eli said again, as if everybody wasn't sniping at each other around us, even though they were trying to lighten the mood.

"And then?" I asked, my voice hollow. Everything hurt and I couldn't think.

"And then you'll find a way to get her back. And we'll show you how to grovel. Because damn it, she deserves more. And so do you."

And at that, my brothers forced me into a group hug, and I was grateful for them. Even though I hated them.

But in that moment, I hated myself more.

Because I hurt her, and I needed to fix this.

I needed to fix it now.

That evening, after talking with my brothers for hours and scheduling an appointment for the next day with my therapist, I drove to Maddie's house, hoping she would see me. I didn't deserve it, but I needed to try.

I had fucked up, so much so that I didn't even know if there was a way out of this, but I needed to try.

I pulled into her driveway, and before I could think about what to say, Maddie was there, standing on her front porch, arms folded over her chest.

"You can just go right away if you're here to hurt me again. I'm doing what I should have done before and standing up for myself."

"Maddie," I said as I got out of the car.

"Don't. Seriously, just don't."

"I'm sorry."

She laughed, but there was no humor in it, only the pain I'd caused. "You're sorry for what? Breaking up with me? Hurting me? Treating me like I was an order that you didn't like at a restaurant and you had to send back to the kitchen? What? What could you possibly say to make this better?"

"I have a lot to work on. I'm not perfect and I never was. But I did the one thing that I promised myself I wouldn't do. I took my trauma and put it on you. I did that two years ago when I stood on that hill and told you that I would never love someone. I was so stupid for doing that, Maddie. I did it because I was scared. I did it because I didn't want to feel what I had been feeling in that moment. And yet I'd said it to the one person that I could hurt the most with my words. I'm sorry. So damn sorry."

"I know you're sorry, but you hurt me. How am I supposed to trust that you're not just going to push me away again when you're scared? Because I could trip and scrape my knee, or do something stupid and get hurt, and I don't want you to push me away and break my heart over and over again because you're scared. I don't know how to fix that, Elijah. But for once, just once, I want someone to put me first. And that might make me a horrible person, but I don't want to be your second choice. I can't be second best."

I moved toward her, grateful when she didn't back away.

"I love you, Maddie."

"Don't. Don't say that. Fuck it. You said it once, and then you walked away. So don't. Don't throw those words out there, as if they're a cure-all."

"I love you. I said what I said because I was scared and I needed to say the cruelest thing that I could so you wouldn't come back to me. Well, it worked," I said with a hollow laugh. "My brothers and I talked and set up an appointment to talk some more as a group. They yelled at me, and I deserved it. We talked about the fact that I'm an idiot, and though I kept saying I was facing my trauma, instead I was just burying it deep down and covering it up with flowers and wine and grape vines and pretending that I was fine. I wasn't fine. I'm not fine. But I am fine with you. You don't heal me. Just like I don't heal you. At least, not in the sense that love fixes all. But it helps. And I was so damn scared of losing you that I pushed you away first. And that was the stupidest thing I've ever done. And I've done a lot of stupid things."

She stared at me. "I don't know what to say to that. I didn't think your brothers would force you to talk like that."

"They are persuasive." I sighed. "I realized that even though I thought I was healed, that I could do anything, I wasn't."

"Because you love Joy."

I shook my head and took her hand. When she didn't pull away, I threaded my fingers with hers, needing her touch.

"I loved Joy. But I'm not in love with her anymore." She opened her mouth to speak, and I cut her off. "Honestly. I'm in love with you. But you're not a replacement for Joy. You're Maddie. I went to Joy's grave the morning of the first day of the festival."

Her eyes widened. "You did?"

I didn't miss the look of hurt on her face, and I cursed.

"I didn't tell you because you were busy, but I was going to tell you and then everything happened."

She nodded, and I continued.

"I went to say goodbye. To tell her about you. And that I was going to tell you that I loved you. And then I got scared. Scared because the last person that I loved died. It was a freak accident, and then look, a flash flood. My mind got a little twisted, and I couldn't break through it. But I'm never going to do that again. I'm never going to let you down like that. That's a promise I can make to you right now. If I get scared, if I get worried, we'll talk it through. I'll do whatever I have to do to prove that to you. I'm sorry for leaving. I'm sorry for hurting you. And I hate myself. But I never want you to doubt me again. I never want to doubt myself. Know that I love you. That I'm sorry. And that I'm working through it. But you aren't my second choice. You aren't second best."

"Elijah." She swallowed hard. "I'm not good at trusting people. I try...and then I break. I can't break again. I don't want to break again."

Tears were streaming down her face. I moved forward and wiped the tears away from her cheeks.

"The man I was before loved Joy. The man that I am now loves you. My heart is big enough for more than one type of love. For more than one type of connection. And I know your heart is big enough to encompass everyone that you come across. You are the light and the peace in our group. You bring happiness and excitement to everything that you do. You are the reason we are who we are. Without you, I don't even think that this company and family would be as connected and operating at the level that we're at. You are the one that pushes us. I want you in my life. And I want to still be in your life. Please, take me back. I love you, Maddie. And I promise I will work to the end of my days to prove that to you. And to make up for everything that I've done. I don't know exactly how yet, but I will find a way."

"I love you, too," she whispered, and my heart squeezed. "I keep telling myself that I need to move away, that I need to leave to make this better, to put myself first, but I love it here. And I hate the fact that my dreams are such a yo-yo sometimes and I can't make a decision. Because I don't know where I am in life, or with you. And I don't want to feel like that anymore."

"Stay. Work for us. Work with us. You are everything, Maddie. Let me be part of your life. Let me love you. That's all I ask."

She was silent for so long, I was afraid she'd walk away. She'd have every right to. But damn it, I'd fight for her. I'd do the thing I *should* have done in the first place.

"I need you to go, Elijah. I need...I need you. I love you. But I don't know how to deal with you leaving. And I hate that I want to forget it happened. But it happened. And I don't know what to do about it."

My heart stopped.

Breaking.

"Anything, Maddie. But I'm not giving up. And I don't want you to. I love you. Don't give up on me."

She met my gaze, the tears falling, breaking me with each passing moment. "I just need tonight, Elijah. To think. I don't think I've done enough of that lately."

And with that, she went inside, leaving me on the doorstep. I knew I needed to do better. To *show* her I wouldn't leave. That I was in this for real.

And I wouldn't leave when things got hard.

Never again.

Chapter Nineteen

Maddie

I stood on a path, staring at a fork in the road and not knowing what choice to make.

And this was so unlike me that I hardly recognized myself.

I hadn't slept well the night before and knew that no amount of peace in my heart would have helped. After everything that had happened with the storm and the aftermath, I should have been exhausted. Instead, I lay awake, wondering if I'd made yet another mistake.

I was good at those.

I stood on the same hill that had once been my solace. The one where I had come daily for years to face the sky and breathe in the world as I tried to come to terms with my days, my dreams, and my choices. The same hill I'd watched Elijah scream at the world when he'd broken.

Where he'd promised to never love again. But he *loved* me. And he wasn't going away. At least, that's what he said. Finding a way to let myself believe that was far harder than perhaps it should be.

"Do you want to talk about it?"

I turned at the soft voice to see Lark standing on the edge of the path. The wind blew her hair in a wavy cascade that made her look like a princess in some fairytale waiting on her prince.

Or maybe she was the one riding into battle, waiting on no man.

That thought made me smile.

"If I can make you smile, I suppose I've done well." She winked as she said it, walking toward me.

"Elijah and I told each other we loved one another, and then I kicked him out of my house because I was still so angry that he left me and thought he could just apologize and all would be well."

I blurted it all nearly in one breath and Lark just blinked at me.

"I'm sorry. I didn't mean to say that. Well, at least not all at once." I ran my hands through my hair, once again annoyed with myself.

"I write love songs. Heartbreak and heartache. I write about hope and promise and all things that come on the path of finding that love. It's not easy to feel it and I've yet to have that all-encompassing love that I see between you two, but from what I've witnessed in my lifetime, however odd it may be, is that sometimes love means breaking down within one another and figuring out what it means to make those promises. And know that there aren't easy answers."

I stared at her, my mouth falling open. "I...you're one of the most beautiful lyricists I've ever had the pleasure of listening to and it sounds like you don't know how to explain love either."

Lark looked at me and burst out laughing. "Right? Love is...special. It's different for everyone and it's different on a daily basis. I want that love. That heart swell that changes a person. But you and Elijah? You have that."

"He left me when it got hard."

And that was the problem. One that I couldn't quite push out of my mind even when he'd promised never to do it again.

"And that was a mistake. And I hate him for you for that."

My lips twitched. "Girl power and everything?"

"You know it. Always. One of the Wilders hurts my girls? I'll break them." She winked. "Or write them into a song."

I grinned. "Oh. Please write a song about the Wilder brothers."

Lark just smiled sweetly at me. "What makes you think I haven't already?"

Intrigued, I leaned forward, but Lark held up her hand.

"If you love him, and if you trust him, then make it work. If you can't do both? Then that's something you need to talk with him about. But you're both hurting, and I hate to see it. I just hope you talk to him. I hate it when people who love and care about one another never talk about the issues between them." Lark sighed. "And I'm done meddling. Be well, Maddie. I'm glad you're safe after the flood." She hugged me tightly and I clung to her, breathing in the fresh air and feeling like I'd finally found my footing.

I knew she was right—I needed to talk to Elijah. And finally make my choices. Because waffling was only making me weaker. And I was never weak.

"I thought you might be here."

I turned at the sound of his familiar voice and my heart sped. It always did that when Elijah was around. "It's my place." I paused. "Or maybe ours."

He smiled at me and it changed his face. He just looked...lighter. As if he wasn't facing his demons daily.

We were both so damn scared of losing each other, we pushed each other away instead.

And at that, I knew my answer. I knew what I wanted.

"I wanted to show you something. If you're free."

I pushed my thoughts away, something hard to do when my entire mindset was changing at the moment. "I'm free..."

"I've been working on something with the winemakers. Sometimes they let me play."

"Jay and Amos are good like that. They won't let me play though...probably because I nearly broke a whole barrel once." Elijah's eyes widened. "Before your time."

"You need to tell me that story."

"I will."

A promise for the future. A hope. And that was a start.

"I've been working with them on something," he paused and took a deep breath, "for you."

My eyes widened. "For me?"

He moved his arm from behind his back, which I hadn't noticed before, but I couldn't help but stare at the wine bottle in his hands.

A Wilder wine that I didn't recognize.

Which made no sense because I knew *all* of the Wilder wines.

"Elijah?"

I didn't mean to make my voice sound so breathy, but there was no taking that back.

"I wanted to make you a batch. I've been working on it forever actually. Before I uh...found the courage to actually do something about it. It's a small batch. One that won't go in stores or wine clubs. Just for our winery here and special occasions. It's a full-bodied yet slightly sweet red blend. One that's perfect for a night with those you love." He let out a breath and tears fell down my cheeks in earnest. "It's Maddie's Home." He laughed at that, and I just shook my head, crying harder. "I tried to find a different name. Something a little catchier, but then you said you were leaving before and I wanted you to come home. To us." He paused. "To me."

I moved to him, unable to hold back. "Elijah...that is the most thoughtful, sweetest, most romantic thing anyone has ever done for me."

"I was going to show you when you signed as partner, but I didn't want to wait. I want you to be home, Maddie. To be with me. And I'll keep finding ways to show you that. Always."

I let out a breath, wiping my tears. "Just never walk away like that again. If you're scared, we talk. But if you ever think about doing that again, it is over. Just like I know if I push you away, it'll be over. We *both* need to do better."

"Deal. Just love me. Take me back."

"I love you, Elijah. I've loved you for far too long. And I know why you did it, why you were scared."

He leaned forward, his body still radiating that tension. "And I'm going to fight. Fight for you, fight for us. Because you deserve that, and more. You deserve everything."

I put my hand on his chest and he relaxed marginally before he lowered his lips to mine and took them, knowing that this was just our beginning. It had to be.

We had messed up more than we could possibly imagine, but we were giving us a second chance.

And it was all I could ask for.

"I guess I'm going to have to call Ivy Wines and Clint to say that I'm staying. They're probably going to think I'm insane."

I hadn't meant to say that, but from the jealous glint in Elijah's gaze, I needed to tread carefully. Not that there was any reason to be jealous. Not with the man I loved.

He narrowed his gaze. "Clint?"

"It's a long story."

He pushed my hair back from my face with his free hand, then kissed me again. I sank into him, loving him more than I could possibly imagine.

"I have all the time in the world for you. So, why don't you tell me?"

"I can do that. And I really want to try that wine." I reached up and kissed him softly and he pulled me close, promising we'd never let go.

And that was a promise we both could keep.

Chapter Twenty

Elijah

The sound of children's laughter filled the air, and I turned to see Evan and Kendall's twins moving around on the grass, scooting and walking as if they had been doing that all their lives, moving far too quickly for my nerves.

Reese and Cassie giggled with one another, Kylie, Eli and Alexis' daughter, only nine months or so younger than the twins, giggled after them.

When Maddie slid her hand into mine, I squeezed it and looked down at her.

"That's a good sound, isn't it?" she whispered.

I let go of her hand so I could wrap my arm around her

shoulders and pull her closer. When I kissed the top of her head, she let out a soft sigh, and I squeezed her as close to me as possible. In the weeks since the flood, and subsequent issues, and since I had groveled my way back into her good graces, we had been taking our time.

We needed to take our time, as it was the one thing we hadn't really done since our road trip.

But here we were, holding one another, and watching as my nieces and nephew laughed and played with one another.

Kendall and Alexis were on baby duty for now, because it was their turn. Of course, I knew that one of my brothers, or Bethany, or even me and Maddie would be in to take over soon. Those kids never were alone, and always had multiple Wilders taking care of them.

It was a little bit chillier today than usual, which was great after the high heats and flash floods. Weather in South Texas never made any sense in any month, but it had been all over the place lately.

"Are you going to help? Or are you just going to stand there?" Evan asked, growling at me. He pointed a hammer at me and I rolled my eyes.

"I guess I should go help put up this stupid thing."

"It's not stupid. It's a pergola. It's gorgeous."

"We have how many outdoor areas? Don't know why we needed this one."

I didn't care, and I liked the pergola, but with Bethany being here more often than not, we had decided we wanted a little space on the property just for family. While I wanted to stay living on the property for as long as possible, not all of us did. So having this space that was just for our use, one we wouldn't rent out, made sense.

East was in charge of everything, since he was an actual certified contractor. So over the past few hours we had put in the rest of the brick work, and were setting up the pergola. By next year the gardens would be overflowing, and there would be play areas and places to sit down as well.

When East wasn't managing all of that, he and Kendall were also working the barbecue. Although me, Maddie, and Elliot helped where we could.

The scent of brisket filled the air and my stomach growled. I knew that the other guests could probably smell it, and they would have their own barbecue, but this piece of brisket was just for us.

"What else are we having?" Elliot asked as he moved around quickly, making sure each of us had our correct tools as I lifted the heavy wood, keeping it in place so East could check his measurements and leveling.

"Potato salad, baked beans, green beans, sweet corn, two different kinds of rolls, four different kinds of pie, baked potatoes that were actually on the barbecue, and corn on the cob that's different than the other corn."

I looked at East, my mouth watering. "Seriously?"

"And of course, brisket, pulled pork, and whole chickens. I thought about doing sausages too, but the pulled pork won in the end. Oh, and also sweet rolls to go with the pulled pork. Kendall and I each made a barbecue sausage you're going to have to judge though."

"My wife's wins," Evan mumbled, and I just grinned.

"I'm starving."

"Are there pickles? Please tell me there are pickles," Bethany asked as she handed over a water bottle.

Everett blanched. "Pickles? As in, you need pickles?" He kept repeating the word and we all looked at her.

She stared at us, before she threw her head back and laughed. "Because onions and pickles and white bread go with barbecue in Texas. You don't need to slather your meat with sauce. And stop making random dick jokes," she warned as I snorted.

"We will always make dick jokes. It's what we do," Everett said as he kissed her nose.

"But yes, we have pickles and onions. But you don't need pickles for any other reason?"

"That's not a dick joke, is it?" she asked, frowning, as I nearly spewed the water that I had just swallowed.

Maddie patted her hand on my back, and I look down at her, rolling my eyes.

"She's not pregnant," Maddie said. "We just want pickles with our food. And I'm not pregnant either. Just putting that out there."

This time I drop the water bottle, spraying water all over us.

"Oh."

"I don't know why you had to scare him like that," Alexis said, shaking her head.

"You know these guys can't handle news like that," Eliza said as she came over the hill.

I did my best to try to wipe the water off my pants before I turned and opened my arms. My sister threw herself at me, hugging me close, before she wiggled down and hugged Maddie as well. "Sorry I'm late."

"I see you just came for the food, pipsqueak," East growled before he kissed the top of her head, and took her from us so he could swing her around.

She laughed and grinned.

"It's just me this time, since the Montgomerys had a thing up north. And I left Lexington up there too."

She scowled at us, as if it was our fault that she was away from her baby.

"Lexington's so big now, and he made me a little care package because he knew he wasn't going to be with me. I'm a horrible mother."

"You're not a horrible mother," Maddie said.

"I just feel like I am. But I wanted to see you guys. And just be the annoying little sister. So much has changed recently, and it's hard to get the family all in one place, so I'm here for a bit."

I smiled at my sister, and at the rest of my siblings.

Things *had* changed. We were all growing, finding our way to settle in these new lives of ours.

I wasn't the same man I had once been, not the man

who had tried to throw myself into building this dream because I had nothing else left. There were no roots, nothing holding me back. Now everything was exactly what I wanted.

I wasn't even the same man I had been two years ago, when I thought I had had my path laid out before me.

Now here I was, my world changing in a whole new way.

And I couldn't wait to see where it went from here.

I looked at Maddie as everyone started talking at once, before we split off to go find our barbecue.

"I love you," I whispered. We had said the words before, but every time I did, I felt like I was screaming it to the world, so everyone knew.

She smiled up at me and brushed my hair from the front of my face.

"I love you too. What's with that look? Is everything okay? Your baby sister's here. You should be happy."

I looked over her head at Eliza and nodded. "I am happy. I'm damn happy. And I have an idea."

She froze. "The last idea you had changed our lives forever. I'm a little worried about what this means."

My lips twitched, before I leaned down and took hers. "Move in with me."

"What?" she blurted, and everyone stared at us. I waved them off, and thankfully the women pulled the guys away, towards the barbecue. Brisket would be the only thing giving us a semblance of privacy.

"Move in with me. And then we can have time to date and see each other. To take our time."

She burst out laughing, and I cringed. "That's not the response I was looking for."

"Elijah Wilder. You want me to move in with you so we can slow down and date like we should have done in the first place?"

"Well, when you say it like that, it sounds weird."

"It's totally weird. We've been dancing around each other in our own way for long enough that it makes sense. And well, I don't think I could ever go back to my home."

A sense of sadness washed over her face, and I squeezed her hands. "I'm sorry, baby."

"I'm sorry too. I loved my home. I loved what I made of it, but it was only supposed to be temporary. I didn't think that I would ever stay here for as long. Not with the people who owned this place before you. And when you moved here, I thought I'd be out on my ass as soon as you guys figured out what you were doing. Or at least figured out how to fake what you're doing. But you guys have thrived here. So have I."

"You're a partner now, baby. You're a part of this."

"Damn straight I am. And you know I told you before that I liked being near the Wilders. Our wines, our barrels. This place. I like being so close. And I like being with you."

"Wait, are you considering moving in with me because

you want to be close to the property?" I asked, only semi-serious.

"That's a big reason in the plus column."

There were so many reasons I loved this woman, and her humor and the fact that she had just said "plus column" were two of them. "Is that a yes?"

"I've always wanted you, Elijah. Even when it hurt me to do so, even when I knew it was a mistake. But I don't want it to be a mistake anymore. So yes, I would love to move in with you. I'd love to take our time and figure out who we are now when we're stepping into these new roles. And I'd love to make a home with you along the way."

I leaned down and softly pressed my lips to hers.

"Thank God you said yes. Because they're all listening, and that was going to be fucking awkward if you said no."

"So awkward, bro," Elliot called out, before he ducked East's fist.

"So, I guess I'm going to be living with the Wilders."

"You've been dealing with us for this long, you might as well continue."

She grinned again. "After all, living with the Wilders would just be coming home. And I want to come home."

"For us," I whispered. "Not for you, not for me, not for the Wilders. But come home for us."

I lowered my head and kissed her again, as the Wilder brothers and sister and everyone else connected to us began to cheer. I just smiled, holding her close.

And when we were pulled apart and taken towards the brisket, and giggling children, and potato salad that made my mouth water, I laughed.

We chose between different sauces, gorged ourselves on way too much food, and found our home.

I had moved here for my own reasons; I had taken a step I never thought I could.

I had loved, lost, sworn to never do either again, and now here I was, taking a chance on fate.

I had fallen in love with Maddie when I hadn't expected it, and I still didn't even know the moment it happened. Only that it had, and I was never going back. I never could go back.

I was a Wilder, but she was my wild salvation.

And this was only our beginning.

Chapter Twenty-One

East

She arched beneath me and I slid my hands down her side, gripping her hips. She moaned, her inner walls clenching around my cock. I kept my pace steady, watching as she writhed beneath me. Her breasts were perfect for my hands, just the right size. Not too big, not too small. Just perfect. I reached down and plucked at her nipples, before I leaned over, sucking one into my mouth. She slid her hands in my hair, pressing me to her breasts, and I moaned against her, sucking, and licking, before moving to bite down on her other one.

Her skin was so soft beneath my fingertips, and it was all I could do not to just pound into her, to need her.

When she writhed on my cock again, I pressed my thumb against her clit, circling it softly at first, and then a little harder, and then even harder until she was coming on me again. I slid out of her, tugging at her hips and flipping her over onto her hands and knees.

She let out a little laugh, one that sounded like bells in my head, and I shook myself, wondering where the fuck that had come from. And then, spreading her cheeks, I slammed into her again, and again, and again. She pushed back at me, her fingers digging into the bedspread, as I fucked her hard from behind, watching the way that her ass jiggled in front of me, the way that her breasts swayed from side to side. She was just so damn fucking beautiful, it was hard for me to breathe. And when she pressed her face down to the pillow, raising her ass even more in the air, I went deeper, harder. She moved back then, looking at me over her shoulder and I winked, surprising myself. I didn't wink in bed. I didn't laugh or smile. Fuck, I did none of that, but with her? For this night?

Why the hell not?

I pulled out of her again, and then positioned us both so I was on my back and she was riding me. She sank down on my cock and shook her head.

"Making me do all the work," she groaned as she rotated her hips.

"Get to it," I growled.

And then she was coming, once again, and I couldn't hold back. I roared, gripped the back of her neck, and pulled her down to me for a crushing kiss. We both shivered as our orgasms finally mellowed, and I did my best not to look at her. I couldn't meet her eyes. Not if I wanted to get away. To walk away. Because that was the one thing that I needed to do. No matter what. No matter if it made me feel like a fucking asshole.

We were both sweaty, out of breath, and I wasn't even sure I could stand. My knees shook, and I lay next to her, both of us naked, and my mouth dry as I tried to catch my breath.

We didn't speak, I didn't think I could. The AC kicked on and the air in the room grew cold. I watched as her nipples pebbled even harder, even tighter, and she slowly slid the sheet over herself.

And just like that, the magic was broken. I sat up.

This was such a mistake. I had known it would be. The first moment I saw her, I knew we would come to this. It was always going to come to this. But it was a damn mistake. I stuffed myself into my jeans and pulled on a shirt as quickly as I could.

I didn't look behind me, but I heard the sound of sheets rustling as she dressed herself. The phone rang beside the bed, and I turned, but it wasn't mine.

Bethany's name lit up the screen and I cursed, before handing over the phone.

Lark looked up at me and shrugged. "I'll call her back."

"You don't have to wait." I knew my voice was gruff, it

always was, but for some reason it sounded even worse now.

"No, it's fine. She can wait a bit."

"So..." I began.

"So..." she continued.

"I guess I should go."

She snorted, her eyes going blank, and her phone held tightly in her hands. "It's your cabin. I should go. But we don't have to talk about it."

I turned to face her, with her gorgeous eyes, her strong cheekbones, the light hair that billowed around her face. She had caught my attention and my breath the moment that I'd seen her, but she was Bethany's best friend, and a God damn celebrity.

People around the world knew her face, listened to her songs, danced to her voice at weddings, and made love under the stars to her sweet tones.

Everybody knew who Lark Thornbird was.

The singer-songwriter who toured the world and was a fucking superstar.

Lark fucking Thornbird.

And I'd done the one thing I told myself I'd never do when it came to her.

"We don't have to talk about it, just don't write a damn song when I leave here."

Her eyes narrowed even as her face paled, and I knew I'd said the wrong thing. But I was done. Done wanting.

Done pretending. Done thinking I could have something I couldn't.

So, as she glared at me, looking as if I had hit her, I walked away, and knew that this was going to bite me in the ass.

Because it always did.

***

NEXT IN THE WILDER BROTHERS SERIES:
East and Lark get their chance in FINDING
THE ROAD TO US.

IF YOU'D LIKE TO READ A BONUS SCENE FROM **ELIJAH**
AND MADDIE:
CHECK OUT THIS SPECIAL EPILOGUE!

A Note from Carrie Ann Ryan

Thank you so much for reading **COMING HOME FOR US.**

I always knew Maddie and Elijah would end up as an HEA. From the start of this series, they were endgame for me.

I didn't know Joy would be there.

And I didn't mean to love Joy. Just like Elijah didn't.

But life, as I know from personal, heartbreaking experience, it's always what we need it to be.

I hope you found the hope that I did with Elijah and Maddie. The love and light that I crave.

And coming up next...I finally get to show you East. He's always that growly guy in the background. And there are reasons for that?

And Lark. Y'all. I love her. And it's time for their story in Stay Here With Me.

The Wilder Brothers Series:

NEXT IN THE WILDER BROTHERS SERIES:
East and Lark get their chance in FINDING THE ROAD TO US.

IF YOU'D LIKE TO READ A BONUS SCENE FROM ELIJAH AND MADDIE:
CHECK OUT THIS SPECIAL EPILOGUE!

If you want to make sure you know what's coming next from me, you can sign up for my newsletter at www. CarrieAnnRyan.com; follow me on twitter at @CarrieAnnRyan, or like my Facebook page. I also have a Facebook Fan Club where we have trivia, chats, and other goodies. You guys are the reason I get to do what I do and I thank you.

Make sure you're signed up for my MAILING LIST so you can know when the next releases are available as well as find giveaways and FREE READS.

Happy Reading!

Also from Carrie Ann Ryan

The Montgomery Ink Legacy Series:

Book 1: Bittersweet Promises

Book 2: At First Meet

Book 2.5: Happily Ever Never

Book 3: Longtime Crush

Book 4: Best Friend Temptation

The Wilder Brothers Series:

Book 1: One Way Back to Me

Book 2: Always the One for Me

Book 3: The Path to You

Book 4: Coming Home for Us

Book 5: Stay Here With Me

Book 6: Finding the Road to Us

The Aspen Pack Series:

Also from Carrie Ann Ryan

Book 1: Etched in Honor
Book 2: Hunted in Darkness
Book 3: Mated in Chaos
Book 4: Harbored in Silence
Book 5: Marked in Flames

The Montgomery Ink: Fort Collins Series:

Book 1: Inked Persuasion
Book 2: Inked Obsession
Book 3: Inked Devotion
Book 3.5: Nothing But Ink
Book 4: Inked Craving
Book 5: Inked Temptation

The Montgomery Ink: Boulder Series:

Book 1: Wrapped in Ink
Book 2: Sated in Ink
Book 3: Embraced in Ink
Book 3: Moments in Ink
Book 4: Seduced in Ink
Book 4.5: Captured in Ink
Book 4.7: Inked Fantasy
Book 4.8: A Very Montgomery Christmas

Montgomery Ink: Colorado Springs

Book 1: Fallen Ink
Book 2: Restless Ink
Book 2.5: Ashes to Ink

Book 3: Jagged Ink
Book 3.5: Ink by Numbers

Montgomery Ink Denver:

Book 0.5: Ink Inspired
Book 0.6: Ink Reunited
Book 1: Delicate Ink
Book 1.5: Forever Ink
Book 2: Tempting Boundaries
Book 3: Harder than Words
Book 3.5: Finally Found You
Book 4: Written in Ink
Book 4.5: Hidden Ink
Book 5: Ink Enduring
Book 6: Ink Exposed
Book 6.5: Adoring Ink
Book 6.6: Love, Honor, & Ink
Book 7: Inked Expressions
Book 7.3: Dropout
Book 7.5: Executive Ink
Book 8: Inked Memories
Book 8.5: Inked Nights
Book 8.7: Second Chance Ink
Book 8.5: Montgomery Midnight Kisses
Bonus: Inked Kingdom

The On My Own Series:

Book 0.5: My First Glance

Book 1: My One Night

Book 2: My Rebound

Book 3: My Next Play

Book 4: My Bad Decisions

The Promise Me Series:

Book 1: Forever Only Once

Book 2: From That Moment

Book 3: Far From Destined

Book 4: From Our First

The Less Than Series:

Book 1: Breathless With Her

Book 2: Reckless With You

Book 3: Shameless With Him

The Fractured Connections Series:

Book 1: Breaking Without You

Book 2: Shouldn't Have You

Book 3: Falling With You

Book 4: Taken With You

The Whiskey and Lies Series:

Book 1: Whiskey Secrets

Book 2: Whiskey Reveals

Book 3: Whiskey Undone

The Gallagher Brothers Series:

Also from Carrie Ann Ryan

Book 1: Love Restored
Book 2: Passion Restored
Book 3: Hope Restored

The Ravenwood Coven Series:
Book 1: Dawn Unearthed
Book 2: Dusk Unveiled
Book 3: Evernight Unleashed

The Talon Pack:
Book 1: Tattered Loyalties
Book 2: An Alpha's Choice
Book 3: Mated in Mist
Book 4: Wolf Betrayed
Book 5: Fractured Silence
Book 6: Destiny Disgraced
Book 7: Eternal Mourning
Book 8: Strength Enduring
Book 9: Forever Broken
Book 10: Mated in Darkness
Book 11: Fated in Winter

Redwood Pack Series:
Book 1: An Alpha's Path
Book 2: A Taste for a Mate
Book 3: Trinity Bound
Book 3.5: A Night Away
Book 4: Enforcer's Redemption

283

Also from Carrie Ann Ryan

Book 4.5: Blurred Expectations
Book 4.7: Forgiveness
Book 5: Shattered Emotions
Book 6: Hidden Destiny
Book 6.5: A Beta's Haven
Book 7: Fighting Fate
Book 7.5: Loving the Omega
Book 7.7: The Hunted Heart
Book 8: Wicked Wolf

The Elements of Five Series:
Book 1: From Breath and Ruin
Book 2: From Flame and Ash
Book 3: From Spirit and Binding
Book 4: From Shadow and Silence

Dante's Circle Series:
Book 1: Dust of My Wings
Book 2: Her Warriors' Three Wishes
Book 3: An Unlucky Moon
Book 3.5: His Choice
Book 4: Tangled Innocence
Book 5: Fierce Enchantment
Book 6: An Immortal's Song
Book 7: Prowled Darkness
Book 8: Dante's Circle Reborn

Holiday, Montana Series:

Book 1: Charmed Spirits

Book 2: Santa's Executive

Book 3: Finding Abigail

Book 4: Her Lucky Love

Book 5: Dreams of Ivory

The Branded Pack Series:
(Written with Alexandra Ivy)

Book 1: Stolen and Forgiven

Book 2: Abandoned and Unseen

Book 3: Buried and Shadowed

About the Author

Carrie Ann Ryan is the New York Times and USA Today bestselling author of contemporary, paranormal, and young adult romance. Her works include the Montgomery Ink, Redwood Pack, Fractured Connections, and Elements of Five series, which have sold over 3.0 million books worldwide. She started writing while in graduate school for her advanced degree in chemistry and hasn't stopped since. Carrie Ann has written over seventy-five novels and novellas with more in the works. When she's not losing herself in her emotional and action-packed worlds, she's reading as much as she can while wrangling her clowder of cats who have more followers than she does.

www.CarrieAnnRyan.com